A Pocket in My Heart

A Pocket in My Heart

Marcia Hoehne

CROSSWAY BOOKS • WHEATON, ILLINOIS
A DIVISION OF GOOD NEWS PUBLISHERS

A Pocket in My Heart

Copyright © 1994 by Marcia Hoehne

Published by Crossway Books
               a division of Good News Publishers
               1300 Crescent Street
               Wheaton, Illinois 60187

Cover illustration: Joy Dunn Keenan

Art Direction/Design: Mark Schramm

First printing 1994

Printed in the United States of America

ISBN 0-89107-781-2

02		01		00		99		98		97		96		95		94
15	14	13	12	11	10	9	8	7	6	5	4	3	2	1

Acknowledgments

I want to thank
Sue Matczynski, Supervisor,
and Marcia Morgan, Social Worker V,
from Child and Family Unit II,
Department of Human Services,
Outagamie County.

Contents

❦ 1 ❦

Chase Scene

"THIS FAMILY IS JUST TOTALLY WEIRD."
Jenna Vander Giffin watched her sister Lia
plant hands on hips and swish her blonde hair
around her shoulders as she stared after their
mother. In seconds Mom, holding Ben's and
Maria's hands, was swallowed up by the booths,
displays, and crowds that thronged the mall this
Saturday afternoon, but Lia continued to stare.

"This family is just totally different from every
other family in the whole world."

Well, that is true, Jenna thought.

"Yeah, but don't you think it's different *good?*"
asked Sherry, their almost-adopted sister.

Lia ignored Sherry and turned back to the
makeup counter. Jenna knew she was looking at
the blush again, trying to decide if she should
wear the pink or peach shades, and the eye
shadow, thinking of the many ways she could con-
tour her lids with plums, russets, and aquas.

"I've been thirteen for two months," Lia grumbled, "and nearly everybody in my class is wearing makeup. Fifteen! Mom said fifteen. I can't believe it."

Jenna had already decided that when her turn came, she was going to get a tweezers first thing and pluck her black eyebrows down to a human size.

"This is all because we're Christians!" Lia tore herself from the makeup counter and jammed her hands on her hips again. She turned her agonized face to Jenna. "Will you please tell me what believing in Jesus has to do with lipstick?"

Jenna sighed. Lia seldom asked for her opinion, and now that she had, Jenna didn't know the answer.

"I just can't wait two years. Honestly, this is totally crazy. I'll be grown up before this family gets anything. Everybody else has air conditioning, a dishwasher, three or four cars—not to mention a back-yard pool."

"We just got a microwave," Jenna said, trying to recapture her chance to influence Lia. "And Dad might be thinking about a computer for Christmas. And as far as the back yard goes, we haven't done too well with stuff out there, have we?"

Jenna felt a nudge of surprise at her own words. After only seven months, she could joke about the

Beautiful Gate! One wistful thought about the playhouse that had burned down passed through her mind. Then eagerness for Lia's response pushed the thought away.

But Lia didn't see the logic of Jenna's words. "Well, I'm not going to just stand here anymore. I've got things I want to see. And I want to be alone, if you don't mind." Lia stalked away, hair swinging behind her. Jenna watched Lia's body take on her usual graceful, fluid motion as she wove between people and disappeared.

I wonder if she'll listen to Mom, Jenna thought, *or if she'll buy makeup and hide it and wear it away from home.* Jenna shrugged. Well, that was Lia's decision. She wasn't about to suggest to Sherry that they tail her and try to catch her painting her lips with Champagne Pink at some cosmetics display. There were more interesting things to do.

"Come on, let's go to the Deb Shop," Jenna said.

After looking at the clothes, they strolled in and out of Record Town and then sighed over lacy nightgowns at Victoria's Secret. At Eye Guys Sherry cried, "Hey!" Then, "Oh, no. I thought for a second that was Amy. You know from school? That girl with the fluffy hair has a jacket just like Amy's."

Jenna looked where Sherry was pointing and saw a golden-haired girl, with her back to them, looking at sunglasses. The girl not only had Amy's jacket, but Amy's medium build and Amy's jeans with the pink heart on the back pocket.

"I wonder," Jenna murmured, catching hold of Sherry's sleeve and circling toward the girl's side. "Amy Van Densen!" Jenna squealed. "You got your hair permed!"

"Oh, hi, guys. Yeah, for the summer." Amy shook her head, and a nest of gold curls brushed her shoulders. "But I'm not sure it's such easy care like they say. This morning I didn't know *what* to do with it."

Jenna imagined her own dark hair molded into smooth, loose curls. But it was so wiry that if she got it permed, she'd probably get in the Guinness Book for having the widest Afro ever recorded.

They left the sunglasses display, and Amy headed down the mall in the opposite direction. Jenna walked backwards, watching Amy's hair puff out behind her shoulders. Amy definitely looked older, even from the back.

"Jenna! You're gonna crash." Sherry grabbed her arm and turned her around. She had nearly smacked into a display case of college T-shirts in the middle of the walkway.

Sherry steered her around Golden Chain Gang. *Sherry is getting more sure of herself*, Jenna thought. She was not the pale, timid girl she used to be. Sometimes, as she had just now, she took the lead.

Jenna herself was seldom comfortable leading, and she felt that she and Sherry were . . . balancing out.

"Oh, let's go to Two Plus Two," Jenna said happily, feeling companionship and respect for her soon-to-be-sister. "I want to look at the earrings, and I'd love to get my ears p—"

"Hey, there's Kate," Sherry broke in.

Jenna scanned the crowd, following Sherry's pointing finger. "I don't see her."

"Behind that tent."

Just ahead of them stood the mall's center stage surrounded by potted plants, and beyond that was pitched a yellow tent across from the Great American Chocolate Chip Cookie Company.

"Kate!" Jenna caught sight of her best friend's coppery hair swishing around her face. Kate looked quickly ahead and then behind. "Kate!" The girls hurried around the stage, around the tent, dodging people, keeping Kate in view. "Kate!"

Kate seemed to be trying to squeeze through the swarm of people boxing her in. Her head darted once more back and forth, and Jenna was surprised to see panic on her face. One hand flew up and slashed hair from her eyes as she caught sight of Jenna.

"Kate!" Jenna tried to reach with her voice without screaming into someone's ear.

Kate's eyes, staring right at Jenna, widened in horror. She turned and dived into the crowd.

"Kate!" Jenna bellowed, unable to believe her own eyes. A dozen people looked at her with annoyed expressions, but she escaped them as she slalomed through the horde of bodies. Her view of Kate was momentarily blocked by a woman carrying a cookie box as big as a billboard. Jenna skimmed past benches and red-on-yellow ad signs, trying to keep Kate in sight. Sherry galloped at her side.

Jenna's senses blurred. The perfume of a styling salon, the rich acrid aroma of fresh coffee beans, the stink of barrel-shaped ashtrays sailed into her nose as she zigzagged to keep sight of a tip of Kate's tennis shoe, or the green waistband of her shorts, or a flash of copper hair. Jenna felt as if she were in a chase scene in a movie and wondered when the mall police would grab them. Suddenly, she realized Kate had disappeared.

In the next instant she slammed into a pillowy body. Her eyes squeezed shut as her nose rammed the woman's chin. In unison Sherry screamed, Jenna cried, "Oohhh!" and the woman bellowed, "What the—" Jenna and the woman hit the floor in a bone-jarring thud, followed by a jangling crash of glass.

"Are you all right, ma'am?" anxious voices asked.

14

"Don't you know any better than that, young lady?" someone scolded.

"You're bleeding," Sherry squeaked to Jenna.

Pushing herself to a sitting position, Jenna felt the blood that trickled from her nose, smearing it with her hand. Her gaze found the woman who lay bewildered on the floor, her grayish hair and her glasses knocked askew. "I'm sorry, I'm sorry, I'm sorry," Jenna whimpered. "Are you hurt? Please don't be hurt bad."

"Maybe we'd better get security," a man's voice said.

"Lady, where are you hurt?"

The woman levered herself up with her elbows. "My hurricane lamp," she finally gasped. "My brand-new hurricane lamp!" She sat up all the way, set her glasses right, and opened the box she'd been carrying. "Now you take a look at what you've done." She held the box toward Jenna, then made an almost sympathetic noise, dug in her purse, and produced a wad of tissues which she shoved into Jenna's hand.

Jenna clutched a tissue over her nose as she peered into the box obediently. She wasn't sure what a hurricane lamp was, but the remains of it looked like a pile of pale pink eggshells.

"Looks like it's been *in* a hurricane," the woman observed. Then she started to laugh. Jenna stared at her.

"Ma'am, are you sure you're okay?" A younger woman leaned over her.

"Well, I think I am, thank you, and I haven't lost my marbles either," the woman said. "I can afford to laugh." She looked at Jenna. "Since the young lady will have to pay for a new lamp. Assuming of course she has wise parents who will make her work for the money instead of just paying for it themselves."

With a sinking heart, Jenna put a new tissue over her nose. She knew her parents were very wise indeed. And she knew she'd soon have to give the names of those wise parents because a uniformed man was striding toward them asking what had happened. The mall police had come to grab her for real.

❧ 2 ❧

Fallout

DO YOU UNDERSTAND HOW LUCKY we are that Mrs. Jarvis is a reasonable woman?" Mom's voice had calmed down to normal, but it still quivered a bit with leftover anger. Jenna had to take giant steps to keep pace with her as they strode toward the mall's main entrance. Sherry, Ben, Maria, and even Lia trotted around them in something like an orbit.

"Lots of people would claim injury and sue us," Mom went on. Small webs of dark hair broke loose from her braid and waved around her head. "She may decide to sue us anyway."

The tempting smells of Cafe Court, of pizza, tacos, subs, and stir-fry faded as they headed out into a pleasant May day. Partly from habit, partly in hopes of escape, Jenna scanned the sky. The clouds looked like double scoops of ice cream. The rows of cars angle-parked nose to nose would look like fish bones from up there. Normally she would have daydreamed for some time, describing things to herself, but today was definitely not normal. Mom's voice brought her right back down to the concrete parking lot.

"The first thing you and I will have to do when we get home is explain to Dad that the checking account is unexpectedly empty because we bought a complete stranger a hurricane lamp."

Jenna winced. Through her memory flashed the picture of the mall officer and bystanders helping Mrs. Geraldine Jarvis to her feet. Then Mom had arrived, summoned by the public address system. Jenna had followed her family and Mrs. Jarvis into J. C. Penney where Mrs. Jarvis had ordered an identical hurricane lamp. Mom had written the check for it, and Mrs. Jarvis seemed fully satisfied.

"I appreciate it greatly," she had said. "More people should take responsibility like you. Most would argue and make excuses for their kid. Fair compensation, that's all I ask." As Mrs. Jarvis had walked away, Jenna had studied her hard to make sure she wasn't limping.

"I sure hope it doesn't turn out that she hurt her back or her leg or something." Mom unlocked the station wagon. Everyone piled in, exclaiming at the stuffiness and rolling down the windows. "Or we could be hearing from her lawyer."

"Oh, I think Mrs. Jarvis had enough padding to cushion her fall." Lia giggled. "What I'd like to know is what Jenna was doing flying through the mall knocking over old ladies. I mean, really, Jenna. What would get you excited enough to run?"

Jenna felt a flash of annoyance with Lia, but the feeling was blotted out by thoughts of Kate. Why had she looked so nervous, so—well, kind of ragged? Why had she turned and run away at the very sight of Jenna, her best friend? Kate was always so bubbly, so friendly and brave and imaginative and just plain fun to be with. Being accepted by someone as popular and exciting as Kate helped Jenna feel good about her own quiet self.

"Hey, wake up, kid. I just insulted you." Lia's finger jabbed her in the back. "Don't you even care? Or didn't you get it?"

"That's enough, Lia," Mom said distractedly.

Mom guided the car up the entrance ramp to Highway 41. Though Jenna loved the smooth speed of a freeway ride, now her mood fell even lower. Friends running away from you in horror meant only one thing, especially when the friends were popular and could be part of any group they wanted. Kate had probably come to the mall with some new friends, kids she'd met at her school or who lived in her town, kids who were more lively and adventurous than plain old Jenna Vander Giffin, kids whom Kate didn't even want Jenna to meet. Kate had fled in terror at the thought that her cool new friends would see Jenna, the dull, dorky kid that used to be her best friend. Jenna slumped.

Oh, Jesus, it's finally happened. Kate met some fun kids, and now she realizes how boring I am. I'm so boring that I don't even know how to do a simple thing like run and find my friend in the mall without causing a major disaster. And now Mom is upset, and Dad will be, too, and I'll have to spend the rest of my life earning $49.95 plus tax to pay Mom and Dad back for the hurricane lamp, and I don't know how I can do that except by doing housework. But maybe it wouldn't seem so bad if I just knew Kate was still my friend!

The car pulled into the driveway long before she was ready.

"Is Dad going to yell at Jenna even though she's big?" Ben asked helpfully.

"A big boy at school knocked somebody down in the hall once and got expended for a day," Maria offered.

"It wasn't your fault." Sherry had pulled herself to the edge of the back seat as the car stopped, and now she whispered into Jenna's neck. Her fingers on the seat back tickled Jenna's shoulder. "It was an accident."

She appreciated Sherry's words, but Jenna felt too distressed to respond. Letting everyone go in ahead of her and then running off somewhere would probably not work. Besides, it was supper time, and she was starving. There was nothing to do but follow them into the house.

❧ 3 ❧

Disaster Dinner

*T*HEY OPENED THE BACK DOOR TO laughter and sizzling and onion-bacon-potato smells. Jenna's stomach fell and then climbed back into place with so much pain she almost groaned.

Dad stood at the stove flipping pancakes. On his curly blond hair perched a chef's hat made from a tube of white posterboard stuffed with a towel that puffed out like a huge, unbaked dinner roll. Across the chest of his white apron a sign had been pinned: *Wunderbar!*

"*Wilkommen*, Frau Vander Giffin and *kinder*," he cried, "to German-Dutch night! In honor of our noble heritage, we have the, ah—"

"*Kartoffel pfannkuchen*," David prompted, pointing to something in a foreign cookbook.

"Ah yes," Dad went on, "also known as potato pancakes. Our salad tonight will be the famous . . . ah, carry on, interpreter."

"*Komkommersla*," David said.

"Dutch cucumbers," Dad filled in. "And as the crowning glory to your dining pleasure, we are featuring the world-renowned German Cherry Torte, Black Forest style. So run upstairs and get into your *klompen* and hurry down to join our *Gemutlichkeit*."

"It smells wonderful, Mark," Mom said.

"That's what the sign says," Dad crowed, tapping the paper on his chest with all ten fingertips. "Just call me Mr. *Wunder*—" Dad finally looked up at Mom's face, and his grin snapped like a broken rubber band. "What's the matter?"

"Let's sit down to eat," Mom said. "But we'll need to have a talk."

Everyone more or less threw their jackets into the closet and filed in. In the dining room, seven-year-old Peter was dealing out forks like playing cards. Cara, who was ten, clunked the milk carton down much too close to the edge of the table. "Hey, you guys. Did you get the part where he said go put on your *klompen*? I bet you didn't know *klompen* was wooden shoes, did you?"

Nobody answered. Jenna hadn't known that, but she thought a word that actually was the sound of the thing it named was a great word, and she might copy it into her journal later. If she felt up to it. She didn't tell Cara she liked the word because Cara, like Lia, always thought she was so important.

"Places, everybody," Dad said.

Everyone sat at the table and joined hands: Jenna to David, David to Dad, then Maria, Cara, Peter, Lia, Tyler, Mom, Ben, Sherry, and back to Jenna. Sherry's hand crept into Jenna's hesitantly and then began squeezing Jenna's fingers so hard her arm bounced. David shot Jenna a look that said, *What in the world kind of trouble did you go and bring home from the mall?*

"Dear God, we thank You for being Lord of our lives and in control of all our circumstances," Dad prayed. "I don't know what's coming here, Lord, but You do, and for that I'm grateful. Help us control our tongues as we speak. Help our communication to be clear and any decisions we make to be in line with Your will. Give us insight through Your Holy Spirit and Your word. In Jesus' name we ask. Amen."

"A-men," everybody said.

"And bless the hands that prepared this meal," Mom said softly.

As David and Lia started the food circulating, Dad said, "What's up? If it's the makeup issue again, you may state your views, Lia, but we're not backing down. And after this one last time the subject will be closed."

"No, that's not it, Mark," Mom said. "Jenna and I have to tell you something that happened at the mall. Jenna, you were there the whole time, and I wasn't. Why don't you explain how it all got started."

Jenna sighed. There was no point in asking to be alone with Mom and Dad. Maria and Ben would blurt the story out at the table anyway, and this way she could tell all the details from her own point of view. So Jenna told her story with lots of background information, lots of details, and lots of apologies. "I'm really sorry it happened, and I'll earn the money to pay you back. I suppose by doing housework or whatever you want me to do." Her voice faded out. She had a sudden mental picture of herself washing the huge living room window with smelly ammonia water and old T-shirts.

She dared to scan the faces of her family as they waited for Dad's reaction. Some just looked sober; some were lighted with amusement; some even wore expressions of quiet glee. David tried to cover a broad grin, but gave up. "*Jenna* got into a *rumble* at the mall?"

This seemed to free everyone to speak.

"Ha-ha, a rumble all right, cool!"

"Jenna, you didn't tell us you joined a gang!"

"Jenna didn't get into a grumble, but Mrs. Jar sure did grumble."

"All right, this isn't helping," Dad said. "We accept your apology, Jenna. You're forgiven, but I want you, all of you, to understand that it was haste and carelessness and poor judgment that led to this accident. You did do wrong, Jenna, by chasing through a crowded shopping mall. I sympathize with your reasons, but I need to know that you know it was wrong so we can be sure it won't happen again."

"It's not her fault!" Sherry yelled, jumping to her feet.

Jenna's head jerked to the right. She stared at Sherry, whose face was nearly purple with outrage. She glanced at the rest of her family, who looked as shocked as she felt. No one had ever imagined in their wildest dreams that timid Sherry might possibly scream at the dinner table.

"It was an accident, and you don't have to yell at her. You are all teasing her, and you are not fair!" Sherry shoved her chair backward and dashed up the stairs.

Jenna remembered last year when she wanted nothing more than to turn off her family's constant noise. Nothing she'd done had succeeded, not the way Sherry had succeeded now. Even Tyler, who was less than two, just stuffed his mouth with Dutch cucumbers, brown eyes staring from a face glazed with syrup and dripping with sweet-sour marinade.

Jenna examined all the half-eaten pancakes around the table—the precisely cut pieces, the doughy shreds, the scalloped edges. Syrup pooled on plates. Cucumber servings sat like little heaps of wet, sliced paper. Only Ben's plate was empty. Only Mom was holding her fork, and she set it down.

"Well, I guess there's two sides to her," David said, still staring up the stairs.

No one answered.

"I'm sorry about supper," Mom said to Dad.

Dad dismissed this with a wave.

"I think something's going on with Sherry. We should call Laurie." Mom crumpled her paper napkin and tossed it onto her plate. "Maybe she can suggest something."

Laurie Joseph was the social worker helping them with Sherry's adoption. Jenna liked her friendliness, but during the meetings and visits she always felt their family was being tested. It was okay for her or her brothers and sisters to think her family was weird, but Jenna did not want a social worker coming in and saying so. Of course, up to now the social worker hadn't. In fact she seemed pleasantly fascinated by the way their family of ten functioned. Jenna wondered how Sherry felt about the interviews with Laurie.

Sherry was happy here, wasn't she? Hadn't she told Lia at the mall that their family was different *good*? Or—wait a minute. Lia had been complaining about the makeup rules. Had Sherry been

26

hinting around to see what Lia thought of the family because *Sherry herself* didn't think it was so hot?

Lia sprang to her feet, light as a cat. "Shall we clear? Maria, you're helping me, I think. Or is it Jenna?"

Jenna raised her eyes to Lia with slow dignity. "I'm on the chart to wash." She strove for a serene alto to contrast with Lia's melodious soprano. "I'm sure Maria knows she is on the chart to clear."

Lia began scraping plates.

"Hey, can't a guy eat?" David grabbed his plate back.

"Those who wish to go may be excused," Dad said. "Those who wish to eat may have that privilege."

"I'll help you clear," Cara offered.

"No, you were on to set," Lia said breezily.

Cara wandered off, casting a few glances at Lia and swishing her blondish-brown hair before disappearing completely.

Jenna wondered if Lia was brushing Cara off precisely because she had captured her. It was true that Cara did not have to clear, but Lia had sung the words in a go-away tone.

Everybody seemed full of surprises lately. Her sisters, even her best friend, seemed to have secret sides to them that nobody expected. *She* didn't, of course. Anything that *she* tried to do that was different from her plain, regular, dull self blew up in her face immediately.

"It's time one of us went up to Sherry," Mom said.

"I will go," Ben declared in his perfect diction.

"No, honey." But Mom probably knew it would be next to impossible to keep him out. Almost nothing happened in the Vander Giffin house apart from four or five people at least. "Put those leftover pancakes in the freezer! They can be microwaved for breakfast," Mom called.

"I'll call Laurie. You go to Sherry," Dad said.

"I don't want any leftover spit-slime pancakes!" Maria whined.

"The whole ones, Maria, not the chewed ones," said Peter.

"Wrapped in foil!" Mom called.

Maria's face brightened. "Hey, I want a piece of woods cake."

"With wax paper between!" Mom called.

"Hey, Dad, what about the woods cake?"

"You mean the German Cherry Black Forest Torte." Ben ripped a pancake lazily down the middle and began to suck both halves.

"Hey, you oughta get this kid a job as the smart-aleck four-year-old on some sitcom." David slurped up one last dripping forkful of syrup. "We could move to L.A. and just lay by the pool while he works and gets rich."

"What do you say we have the dessert later as kind of an evening snack?" Dad said.

"Now, now, now," chanted Peter, Maria, and Ben.

"Nope." Dad got up and strode to the den and closed the door. Though she couldn't hear above the complaining, Jenna was sure he picked up the phone.

Mom went upstairs. Jenna headed to the kitchen and found a greasy bacon pan, a cherry-smeared saucepan, and three mixing bowls all wedged into the sink among eleven sticky plates. The whole mound bristled with silverware.

"Where'm I supposed to fit the water?" she asked.

"Jenna, don't you just *wish* we had a dishwasher at times like this?" Lia was trying to stuff something into the refrigerator.

"Times like this happen three times a day," Jenna said.

"Exactly. Ben, get your fingers *out* of that dessert. Go play someplace. Just think, Jenna. Instead of standing there scrubbing at those gross things, you could just flip a switch and get on with your life."

Jenna looked at the pile in the sink, willing it to vanish.

"And they get cleaner, too, because of the scalding hot water it can use. You'd think Mom and Dad would go for that sanitary stuff, wouldn't you?"

"Yeah." Jenna sighed.

"Maria, we're gonna need the vacuum for that." Lia turned to Jenna again. "She's trying to sweep up about eight pounds of chocolate sprinkles with that half-bald broom. That dessert has 'em stuck all over the sides of it, can you imagine? Honestly, I'll bet David stood ten feet from the cake and threw handfuls at it. Anyway, as I was saying, I'll share a little secret with you." Lia smiled and sidled close to Jenna's right ear. "I'm really feeling . . . constrained lately by Mom and Dad's rules. When you're a teenager, you've got to become your own person, find your own place in the world. Do you understand?"

Jenna nodded.

Lia sighed hugely. "Oh, thank you, Jenna. I knew you would. Anyway, so many of the decisions they make affect us. You know what I mean?"

Jenna nodded. "Like they won't buy a dishwasher, but *we* have to do the dishes."

"Right," Lia said. "Well, I'm going to do something about it. Take the dishwasher as an example. It would take me less than a year to save up for one."

"You're gonna *buy* one?"

"Ssshhh." Lia laughed. "You bet. *On my own.* And that's only one example."

"Wow," Jenna said. Maybe if Lia, who did quite a lot of baby-sitting, could afford a dishwasher in a year, she herself could pay off a hurricane lamp in that time by doing housework. Jenna wished she could baby-sit, but Mom and Dad had this stupid rule that baby-sitters had to be twelve. She sighed. The idea that it might take a whole year to pay Mom and Dad back was too much to bear.

"I'm telling you this because I would value your support," Lia whispered. "And you might want to be thinking how this affects your own life."

Jenna nodded. To think this graceful, vivacious sister would need *her* support. "Thanks, Lia."

"Thank *you*, Sis."

"Jenna."

The girls were startled and whirled to the doorway as one.

"I was just about to run the water," Jenna said.

Mom held up her hand. "I've been trying to talk to Sherry, but she's asking for you."

"Me?"

"Um-hum."

Curiosity bloomed in Jenna. The sink full of dishes caught her eye, and her spirits rose at the thought of escaping them after all. She started forward.

"Oooohhh, yuuuckk!" Lia and Mom howled.

Jenna looked back. Peter, Maria, Ben, and Tyler were down on all fours with tongues protruding, like so many anteaters, licking chocolate sprinkles off the floor.

❦ 4 ❦

Secrets

Y OUR PARENTS THINK THEY'RE SO good."

Jenna had barely closed the door of their room, and she sank against it, stunned. She had expected to find Sherry mute, maybe sniffling, curled up on her bed. Instead she sat on it with arms crossed, glowering through her hair. What was Sherry so angry about? She seemed to have too much rage for anything that had happened.

"Sherry . . . it's not so bad. It won't be much fun paying Mom and Dad back, but they're not doing anything else to me. Why are you so mad?"

Sherry crossed her arms even harder and bounced on the bed. "Oh, what do you know about it? Maybe I want Lia instead."

"Sherry! First you were mad *for* me, and now all of a sudden you're mad *at* me! What did I say?"

Sherry pulled her eyebrows together even farther.

Jenna wondered how Sherry could want Lia when it was the two of them, Jenna and Sherry, who had become close. Unless . . . unless Sherry wanted somebody lively and talkative and always flouncing around, like Lia. Unless Sherry realized that Jenna was no good when it came to knowing the right thing to say. Could it be that her new sister as well as her best friend had found out that Jenna Vander Giffin was as dull as dishwater?

Jenna took a deep breath and asked a hard question. "Do you want me to get Lia for you?"

"No," Sherry grumped. She answered so quickly that Jenna was sure Sherry hadn't really wanted her. What kind of game was Sherry playing?

Sherry lifted her chin and shook the curtain of hair away from her eyes. "Did you ever think, I mean, if you're going to get in trouble even for accidents that you might as well just be bad? You're gonna get in trouble anyway."

Jenna stared at Sherry. Her voice was calm enough, maybe too calm. Her face was also calm, but her eyes held a new sharp light.

"Well, no," Jenna said, thinking she must sound duller than ever. "But I guess I know what you mean, in a way." Jenna's voice faded out as she began to think about being bad on purpose. Was that what a person would do if people *thought* she was bad, even if she had only done wrong by mistake?

"Sherry? You're not going to—Sherry, Mom and Dad don't think you're bad."

Sherry arranged her lips in a tight line, and her eyes grew bright and quivery the way they always did when she was going to start shifting them around.

"Sherry." Jenna worked up her courage to try one more time. "What's the matter? I don't understand. You've always liked it here, haven't you? Why did you call Mom and Dad 'your' mom and dad? They're yours, too. Your adoption is going to be final next month!"

"Maybe I don't want to get adopted. Maybe I don't belong in your stupid family."

"Sherry!" Jenna felt her mouth hanging open with hurt.

"Well, it's true."

"You're already my sister."

"Nuh-uh."

"Well, you must be!" Jenna exploded. "You're finally acting just as dumb as everybody else in this family!"

Sherry's eyes, still quivery, stared at Jenna. Jenna didn't know if she wanted Sherry to fight back or not.

"I'm sorry," Jenna said.

"I don't want to talk anymore."

"I didn't mean to hurt your feelings."

"Forget it. I just mean I want to be done talking now."

"Okay." Jenna left the room, shutting the door behind her.

If she went down to the kitchen, she might have to finish the dishes, so she sat at the top of the staircase, a girl without a room.

Lia and Sherry and Kate had done such surprising things lately. For Lia life had always been a soprano solo, a twirling skirt, long swinging hair, and a dainty leap as she flew from here to there laughing her musical laugh. Now she spent half her time complaining and was planning to declare her independence from the family rules by buying everything from makeup to major appliances.

Sherry had always been shy, needing her family's love more than anything in the world. Now with her shaggy blonde hair, her sharp thin face, and a new fire in her eye, she reminded Jenna of the tough, scary kids at school who smoked and wore black T-shirts with skulls on them.

And Kate. Her bubbly, kind, exciting, reassuring, pretty—she could go on and on—friend Kate. Today Kate had seen her unexpectedly and had fled from her as if she were all the plagues of Egypt rolled into one.

Lia, Sherry, and Kate all had secret sides that

people might not know were there. But did she, Jenna Vander Giffin, have such a secret side? No. Everybody expected her to be quiet and dull, always well behaved, nose buried in a book or her journal. Oh, if she knocked old ladies down in the mall, people were surprised, sure. But such awful, stupid, and embarrassing disasters did not add up to a secret side.

A secret side would mean people wouldn't know her completely. She could have an independent pocket in her heart that would surprise people if she ever opened it. It would make people say, "Oh, Jenna is endlessly interesting. A fascinating young woman, really."

A secret side would mean people couldn't own her completely—people like her parents. Come to think of it, they did always insist on the rules. They did always keep track of everybody's business. And they always expected her to be a child who wouldn't give them any grief. Maybe if parents expected you to be too good, that would make a kid want to cut loose, too? Jenna pondered this idea carefully, getting up only when the step became too uncomfortable for her bottom.

She had to call Kate. She had to ask her what was wrong, what she had done, what she could do to make things better between them again. Kate would forgive her. She had never been mean to

Jenna in their lives. Then Jenna could talk to her about secret sides and ask Kate how to get one.

Better than that, she could *observe* Kate, kind of—well, not spy really, but study her. She could imagine delving under Kate's skin, into her head, below the bones, and being that self that was Kate, possessing the secrets. Were other people really selves like she was, inside their bodies?

Jenna couldn't really picture it, but she guessed they must be. Because if anybody could show her how to develop a fascinating, surprising, secret side of herself, it would be her exciting, clever, helpful, cool friend Kate.

❦

"You know I didn't see you at the mall now, right?" Kate said. "You must have seen me when I was running to J. C. Penney to meet Mom. I had just found out I was twenty minutes late and knew she'd be upset."

It was Sunday afternoon, and Jenna and Kate had just closed the door to Kate's room.

"Yeah, you explained that yesterday on the phone." Jenna supposed it could seem that a person was looking right at her when she was really looking past her or over her head, but a trace of doubt clouded her mind. "Did you get your ears pierced at the mall, too?" Jenna admired the small amber stones set in gold that twinkled just at the edge of Kate's stylish, chin-length hair.

"Yeah, but that was Thursday, not yesterday. It was a present from my dad when he got back from his business trip. He bought Jason a phone for his room."

An odd longing stirred Jenna's stomach. No matter how well she knew Kate, her friend kept spurting ahead of that knowledge in small, surprising ways. Why hadn't Kate called her on Thursday and told her right away about her pierced ears? But it was just this kind of secret side that Jenna needed her to have. Jenna shook her confusion aside, knowing that when she'd come to Kate, she'd come to the right place.

"About yesterday," Kate said. "It was a miracle you saw me in that crowd. It would have been a double miracle if I'd seen you. I just want to be sure you aren't mad or anything. I can't believe you'd think I'd make a face at you and run away. I'd never do that. You're my best friend!"

Mollified, Jenna smiled at Kate. With her bouncy copper hair, gray eyes, gleaming white smile, and sunny disposition, Kate reminded Jenna of Anne of Green Gables. Wasn't it a fantastic blessing to have a sort of Anne of Green Gables of her own? Jenna wondered if the high school or community players would ever put on Anne of Green Gables as a play. Kate would be the perfect Anne, and Jenna would be her devoted dark-haired friend, Diana. Maybe they should start growing their hair long now.

"Can we climb up on your bunk?" Jenna asked. Whenever they got together at Kate's, their habit was to go up on her top bunk and toss the ladder to the floor.

"Well, sometimes I think that's kind of babyish now." Kate eyed the bunk. "Especially the ladder part. I mean, we know nobody's going to climb after us." Her voice became suddenly brisk. "Never mind. Let's go up there."

They mounted the ladder and swung their legs over the footboard. Ordinarily Jenna would have detached the ladder immediately and sent it plummeting to a satisfying thud on the carpet. To her the action stood for their plan to be alone, to keep everyone else away from their delicious secrets, even though the ladder really had nothing to do with whether people interrupted them or not. But this time Jenna didn't touch it.

"We can take it down." Kate knocked the ladder off the end of the bed rather crookedly. "Maybe we better take it down." She looked at Jenna. "I've got a pretty big secret."

Jenna had been about to ask Kate if she'd seen any of the commotion with Mrs. Geraldine Jarvis and her hurricane lamp, since it had happened near J. C. Penney. But she wiped this right out of her mind. "What secret?"

When Kate didn't answer right away, Jenna went on. "I've got one, too. I've got to earn some pretty big money, and I need you to help me think how to do it."

"I think my parents are getting a divorce," Kate broke in.

Jenna turned to her, amazed. Kate's face was perfectly somber, and she was staring down at her peach and apple-green plaid bedspread.

"Did they say they are? Do they fight?" Jenna asked.

"All the time, when Dad is home. But Dad's usually not home. That's what they fight about. Did you ever hear of a workaholic?"

Jenna wrinkled her brow. "I guess so." She had never thought much about what the word meant.

"My mom calls him that. She says Dad is so wrapped up in his job he doesn't have time for his family. She says when he does come home, he changes her rules and spoils us with too many presents."

"Kate? This probably sounds stupid, but—what does your dad do?"

"I don't really know. Doesn't *that* sound stupid? He works at Morgan & Lee. He's called an account executive."

Jenna had never heard of either Morgan & Lee or account executives.

"I know they do advertising, and my dad tries to keep a lot of customers happy. My dad tells my mom that all he does is for other people—his customers, the church, our family—and still everybody's unhappy with him. Then my mom complains he does nothing for his family. My dad argues that he knocks himself out to provide for us, and they start fighting again. My mom thought maybe she should get a job so he can work less, but then she said he'd work just as much no matter what she does. She says somebody has to be home to be a parent." Kate paused, still looking at her bedspread. "You know what?"

Jenna watched Kate anxiously. She'd never seen Kate so gloomy before.

"If they didn't have Jason and me, well—" Kate's voice began to waver, and she turned toward the wall. "It wouldn't matter so much that my dad has to work a super lot, and my mom could work, too, instead of feeling like she has to sit here with us."

Dismayed, Jenna waited for Kate to make the next move.

Kate turned back suddenly, making her hair swish around her face, and smiled a faint version of her usually beaming smile. "Well, what did you want to tell me? Tell me the whole thing with all the details. Every single one."

Jenna again told the story of Mrs. Geraldine Jarvis and her hurricane lamp. Kate made comforting, horrified noises in all the right places and never once laughed over her clumsiness or shrieked, "Jenna, *you* did that?" She even looked mildly uncomfortable by the time Jenna had finished.

"This all happened because you were trying to catch me?" Kate asked.

"But it's not your fault. You didn't see me. I just didn't watch where I was going."

"Right," Kate said softly.

"Anyhow, I need to raise money. Any ideas?"

"We could walk Mrs. Clement's dogs. She just lives two houses down, and she'll pay a dollar per dog. She's got two dogs that look like sheep, but closer to the ground. They're even named Fleecy and Woolly."

"Okay." Jenna was willing to walk the dogs, but she wasn't quite ready to come down from Kate's top bunk. She hadn't raised the subject she really wanted to discuss.

Somehow she couldn't make herself come out and ask Kate if she'd ever wished for a secret side. Maybe that was because it seemed Kate did have a secret side now, a side bigger than pierced ears, a side that included family problems nobody had known were there. Kate had begun to smile and act like her old self though as soon as she'd finished telling the story about her parents. She must be okay. Everyone knew that Kate Schmidt was always lighthearted and ready to take on the world. All Jenna had to do was spend the afternoon with her, learning from her, and she'd have the key to her own adventurous, humorous, popular, and unboring secret life.

❧ 5 ❧

Acting Out

"MOM, WHAT'S MY BIBLE VERSE FOR today?" Maria asked.

Mom consulted the Sunday school take-home paper stuck to the refrigerator. "'I praise You because I am fearfully and wonderfully made.' Can you say that?"

"I praise You," Maria chirped, "'cause I am a wonderful maid."

The first real laughter in twenty-four hours rang through the kitchen. Maria, dressed head to toe in pink, including hair ribbon and ballet slippers, pirouetted around the room holding a plate of bread. Lia came in the back door then, shaking her hair and hanging up her jacket.

Watching her, Jenna giggled, thinking how the house was just full of wonderful maids. But Lia tossed her a wink and a smile as she walked through, and Jenna, suddenly remembering the secret they shared, felt confused and shut off the giggle. She finished tossing the salad and looked for someone to hand it to. Who was on to set tonight anyway?

"Ha-ha, you heard her," Peter called as he trotted by. "She's a wonderful maid so she's gotta do all the work."

"Yeah, that was a pretty dumb thing to say," Cara agreed.

"I don't think a servant is the kind of maid Maria had in mind." Amusement still tinged Mom's voice. "Hey, why is everything piling up out here? Where are our table-setters?"

"Uh-oh, uh-oh, uh-oh," Cara chanted, heading to the closet door to inspect the job chart. "Sherry's on to set. And David."

"David won't be here. Senior high youth group is stopping at McDonald's," Mom said.

"Oh yeah, he traded with me!"

"Okay then, Cara, you're on. Where's Sherry?" Everyone looked at everyone else.

"Somebody's gonna get her allowance docked," Cara sang.

Mom pursed her lips, headed to the stairs, and called Lia down to do Sherry's job.

"Honestly, Mom, that's not fair!" Lia gripped the upper banister with both hands, hair cascading over one shoulder.

"Sherry will either have to do a job for you or pay you the same amount she gets docked," Mom told her. "And as touchy as she's been with Dad and me lately, I'd really rather she didn't owe one of us for the job."

Jenna followed Mom into the dining room, salad bowl in hand. "I'll do it." She couldn't believe Mom hadn't asked her first. Everybody knew she needed money because of Mrs. G. J. and her lamp. The words, "I'll do it," left her mouth at the very instant Lia's eyes gleamed at the word *pay*.

Lia flashed a look of offended surprise at Jenna and still managed to keep her tone aggrieved. "Never mind. I'm here." She descended the staircase at medium speed.

"I guess I automatically thought of someone who didn't have a job right now." Mom looked at Jenna half apologetically and disappeared back into the kitchen.

For the first time Jenna realized that both she and Lia were trying to earn money, and only her own efforts were public. In exchange for the privilege of knowing Lia's secret, would she be expected to make sure Lia got a share of the jobs offered to her?

"Boy, Sherry never missed a job before." Cara passed out plates.

"It's a relief to see she's a normal kid," Lia said. "Not such a . . . puppy."

"Lia," Mom objected.

"I know, I know. But when somebody just kind of hangs on you and wants to please you every minute, isn't it kind of pathetic?"

"With foster children that's called the honeymoon period," Mom said.

Lia, Jenna, Cara, Peter, and Maria looked at her.

"They're 'too good' at first because they're afraid of rejection. Sherry's honeymoon has been extremely long. Maybe she's been so eager to become one of us that she's ignored any mixed feelings. Unfortunately, the next period is usually rebellious. They're testing the family's commitment to them. Just remember, try to understand, that she may be disobedient because she's testing us." Mom sighed. "Because I think we may be in for kind of a rough ride."

Sherry couldn't have hoped to sneak in. She had to know that by 6:30 supper would be cleared away, and the ten Vander Giffins spread like a dragnet over the house. Dad was in the den doing lesson plans for his high school technology classes or church work or something. Mom was in the living room reading a tower of books to Ben, Tyler, and Maria, and listening to Peter read from his first grade reader. Cara and Jenna sat at the dining room table, laying open textbooks and wrinkled papers end to end and chasing rolling pencils over the surface.

The back doorknob turned. The door brushed over the weather-stripped threshold and swung open in that brief squeak like a horse's whinny. They all knew without looking that it was Sherry, but Jenna and Cara, who could see the door from the table, looked anyway.

Mom, trailed by Ben, Tyler, Maria, and Peter, came through the dining room and met Sherry in the doorway to the kitchen. Sherry's face closed, but Jenna had seen the round eyes and tight lips before they went dull and slack.

"Sherry, are you all right? We were terribly worried when you didn't come home for supper. What happened?"

Sherry said nothing, but her glance flickered toward the doorway to the living room, and Jenna knew Dad was standing there.

"Honey, we were worried," Mom said.

Sherry gazed past Mom, hiding behind her own blank expression.

"If you have no good reason, you know there'll have to be consequences."

"Yeah, you gotta pay Lia for setting the table for you," Maria piped up.

"You have done a double triple no-no," Ben advised.

"Kids, upstairs." Dad herded them up and

joined Mom and Sherry in the doorway. "Sherry, if you have anything to tell us, now's the time."

Her shoulders shrugged the tiniest bit, but Sherry stayed mute.

"Okay," Dad said. "We'll have to restrict you to the yard for three days. If we can't trust you to be home on time, you're not responsible enough to go out."

"Your allowance will be cut because you missed your job," Mom added, "and you know you'll either have to pay Lia or take her turn at a chore."

"Lia will choose the pay." Cara erased frantically and tore an accordion rip in her worksheet.

Jenna wondered why some people couldn't see when it was smart to keep quiet. Fortunately, Mom and Dad ignored Cara's remark instead of sending them away. She noticed though that Cara was aware of Lia's recent interest in money.

"You can't take the money." Sherry aimed her eyes nearer to Mom and Dad. "You get paid to take care of me. You have to spend the money on me."

"And we do," Dad replied. "That doesn't mean we hand all of it over to you."

"You just keep me here for the money!"

"Sherry, we are going to *adopt* you." Mom reached out a little, but Sherry ignored her hand. "We're your *parents* now."

"You can get money for that, too! I know,

'cause Laurie said." Sherry's face reddened. "You can get a—susbidy . . . sussity . . . see, it's true 'cause I know the word even. If you couldn't still get the money, you wouldn't adopt me."

"That's not true," Dad said.

"Is too. You know, I don't have to stay here like your kids do. I didn't come out of your stomach, and I can leave if I want to." Sherry headed for the stairs.

"You're our daughter," Mom called after her, softly. "And we'll always be your family no matter what."

The answer was a slammed door.

Jenna sat in silence, the kind that went beyond sound to muscles and bones and breathing. Cara's neck remained twisted toward Mom and Dad, who gazed up the empty stairs. Jenna couldn't feel how they felt, but she saw with astonishment their yearning.

"What more can we say?" Mom asked softly. "What more can we do to assure her?"

We're not here, Jenna realized. For Mom and Dad, she and Cara weren't there in the room.

"It's a stage she has to go through," Dad answered. "And she'll go through it and come out on the other side."

"I'm scared, Mark."

"Maybe not as scared as Sherry." Dad's voice was no stronger than a murmur. "We're her third family. The first two both gave her up. I'd say she's daring us to let her down now if we're going to, to not lead her on any longer if we're only going to disappoint her."

"Then the only thing to do is to show her that will never happen," Mom said.

"We stand firm. We pray and we stand firm."

"You will never, ever be abandoned again," Mom said fiercely, softly, still looking up the stairs. "Never again."

They turned and saw the girls.

Cara jerked back to the table and began coloring her relief map of Wisconsin. Colored pencils rolled and bounced off the chairs.

Jenna didn't move. Her eyes met Mom's, and she kept them there, wanting to signal that she would be silent, that she needed nothing from them now at all. Then she slowly lowered her head to her work, found a pencil with a point on it, and strained through the task of filling a sheet with long division of decimals.

"Jenna? Come up and talk awhile."

It was Mom on the stairs. Jenna suddenly remembered that it was time for their personal half-hour together. Mom had read that some long-ago lady named Susanna Wesley spent half an hour every week with each of her nineteen children. Mom had figured that if Susanna could do it with nineteen, she could do it with nine. Jenna wondered if Mom wanted to discuss Sherry, or her money-raising efforts, or her visit with Kate, and if she'd been listening at the head of the stairs for the sound of Jenna's math book slapping shut.

"Was the math tough?" Mom closed the door of Dad's and her room behind them. Jenna bunched up the comforter at the foot of the bed and curled against it while Mom stood at the mirror, unwound her braid, and pulled a brush through her hair.

"The math is always tough." Jenna groaned. "Hey, your hair looks nice."

Jenna meant it, but in a way she was surprised she thought so. She knew she (and Maria) had inherited Mom's hair. Right now it puffed out from Mom's head as if she had a natural body perm, but Jenna had always thought she could use her own to scrub pots.

Mom laughed. "I don't look too much like a lion? Thanks, hon. Actually, I've been thinking of getting it cut. What do you think?"

Cut? Well, she guessed that would look more up-to-date, but Mom was the only person who could look so right in a braid. Of course it helped that she was thin in her jeans and naturally pretty in an unfancy way. Jenna was about to reply that a cut was a good idea and then maybe steer the conversation to what she might do about her own looks, when Mom spoke again.

"I told Lia she could get her ears pierced."

Jenna rose up from the comforter, electrified. "Does that mean I can, too?"

"Well," Mom said carefully, "no, it doesn't." Her brushing arm slowed down.

"Why not? I've wanted to get them pierced for a long time." Jenna knelt as tall as she could, letting go of the comforter, and her voice came out anguished. "Why is Lia different?"

"Oh, honey, she just needs to distinguish herself a little now. We told her that anyone over age twelve could get her ears pierced so that she could feel she was the first to get the privilege." Mom turned to Jenna. "I hope you and the other girls will understand."

"So there's a rule now that you have to be twelve to get your ears pierced?"

"I suppose you could put it that way." Mom set the brush down.

Jenna wondered what was so magic about age twelve that baby-sitting and ear-piercing had to wait till then. She would be twelve in eight months. Wasn't that close enough? And why on earth did Lia need to *distinguish* herself? She already caught the eye of everyone around with her vivacious personality, her artistic talents, her flowing-haired beauty.

Her beauty. That was why Lia wanted to wear makeup, of course. She would be more beautiful than all her friends, and she would get all the boyfriends and all the attention. Maybe Mom had decided it would be a shame not to let her. Maybe Mom also thought that for plain old wire-haired, bushy-eyebrowed Jenna there was no reason to bother.

Jenna looked up to see Mom watching her fondly.

"Your thoughtfulness is one of the things I enjoy about you, Jenna. I know you. I know I can always count on you to think things through and to understand, at least as far as you're able."

Jenna's heart jolted. Usually she loved her half-hours with Mom. They would discuss school or the latest book Jenna had fallen in love with or her new hobby of baking. But now she knew for sure that all her fears about being the knowable, reasonable, predictable Jenna were true. She felt duller and younger and more controllable than ever. The half-hour couldn't end too soon. She was angry with Mom for causing all these sensations.

"I imagine you had fun visiting Kate," Mom commented.

"Sure," Jenna said automatically.

In reality Jenna felt mixed up about her time with Kate. Walking Fleecy and Woolly, they'd been hauled down the street side by side in stiff, slapping steps by two curly-haired bundles of muscle. Their arms had pulled parallel, elbows straining, to hold the taut leashes, and Jenna had felt their sameness. She'd felt she could almost cross over into Kate, and the key to having a secret side could be embedded in her own store of knowledge.

"If these dogs swim as fast as they walk, I could water-ski." Kate suddenly grabbed Fleecy's leash, and Jenna let go. Kate planted her heels and tried to skid along the walk, arms curved like a wishbone. She laughed delightedly. "Maybe if there was gravel under my feet, it would work."

"I'll find some." Jenna scanned the street and nearby driveways for small pebbles, but only perfect gray-white concrete flowed and sloped over curbs and arced up to garages. Kate's was not a gravel type of neighborhood.

"Forget it. No big deal." Kate pushed Fleecy's leash into Jenna's hand absentmindedly. Her attention had been caught by the corner brick house, which was tall and had a stone arch entry and red double doors. Anticipation spread over Kate's whole face. "Damian Hochhauser studies in there." Smiling impishly, she focused on a bay window and sprang up on tiptoes, trying to see inside.

Jenna followed suit.

"No, Jenna, come on, don't you do it, too!"

Thunderstruck, Jenna turned to Kate. She saw nothing but copper hair as Kate trotted after Woolly. She'd been shocked to find herself wondering if the key to a secret side was rudeness.

Now, thinking about Kate, sitting here with Mom, Jenna caught her breath as she realized something. Mom didn't seem to know about Kate's parents getting a divorce. If she knew, Mom would have brought it up. The words rushed to Jenna's tongue, but she deliberately swallowed. Then she rubbed her tongue on the roof of her mouth for good measure.

"Is something wrong, hon? You seem a little distant."

Jenna shook her head. She even managed to give Mom a smile because she had just discovered secret knowledge inside herself that Mom did not possess—knowledge that had come from Kate. This was proof that creating a secret side meant listening to Kate until all the tricks seeped into her. Getting together often with Kate wouldn't be easy because of the distance they lived apart. She might even be nervous after today. Kate had said good-bye with a very distracted, "Call you sometime." But one thing about Kate—she didn't worry too much.

She would call Kate tomorrow after school and suggest they go on an adventure. Kate would know what kind. Kate loved excitement and would come up with an idea in two minutes, tops. The key to a secret side was to go out and have experiences, to try Kate on for size somehow. She was on her way to being a new, exciting, unpredictable Jenna!

❧ 6 ❧

How to Be Mysterious

JENNA STEPPED OFF THE BUS AT Kate's corner and felt a whoosh of relief swoop through her at the sight of Kate watching from her front yard. She thrust her arm up in a high, sweeping wave, brushing away her uneasiness about Kate's lack of enthusiasm when she'd asked to come over. She jogged up to Kate's house, smiling broadly. "Why didn't we ever think of this before?"

"The bus, you mean?" Kate's tone was polite, as if she didn't understand Jenna's merriment and really needed an explanation. "They didn't consider us old enough before."

"They hardly do now either." Jenna made a face. "My mom asked a hundred questions about how close the bus stop was to your house, and was I sure, and then she had to check the bus map, and how did I plan to get home because the buses would stop running by then. She asked if I expected her to pay the fare since I probably wanted to save my money for Mrs. Jarvis and her lamp. She asked if I had homework." Jenna's voice began to take on a singsong tone. "I told her on early-release days they don't give homework."

"Is that true?" Kate asked.

Jenna looked at Kate with some surprise. Kate's head was tipped in an unfamiliar gesture, and she raked her wriggling fingers through her hair on that side.

"Yeah, it's true."

"What do you want to do?"

Jenna took a breath. "Well, I've got something for the top bunk. Is that okay? We don't have to throw the ladder down or anything." She paused, looking at Kate's house. "We don't even have to go up there if you don't want. Outside is okay. Maybe when I say I've got something for the top bunk, it'll just be a signal that I've got a secret."

There had been other signals in their friendship. Jenna remembered the time Dad had told them that people in the early church drew fish symbols to recognize each other. If one person drew half a fish, and the person he was meeting drew the other half, they knew they were both Christians and could talk about Jesus without getting in trouble with the authorities. For a long time after they heard this story, Jenna and Kate drew fish symbols whenever they met. One would draw the first curved line, like an eyebrow, and the other would add the bottom line, which curved up and formed a pointed head at one end and a crossed tail behind. Then they would fall together in relieved abandon and spill all their secrets. And they would have died of embarrassment to share their fish symbols with anybody.

Kate hadn't spoken. Jenna found herself still staring at Kate's house. The Schmidt home wasn't enormous, but it had two stories and was built in a style that had a name. It was a silly royal-sounding name that made her think of butlers and plump ladies dripping diamonds and made her want to giggle. *Tudor*, that was it. The house was a red-brown color that Lia had pronounced mahogany, with three kinds of siding—stucco, brick, and wood. The large windows were made up of little squares, and one of them had a rounded top and an iron balcony railing in front of it. There were two fireplace chimneys, well-groomed puffballs of green shrubbery, and a thick, gently sloping lawn. Although all of the houses were different, the whole neighborhood was beautiful like this. These were the kind of homes where people had the latest stuff, where they relaxed in whirlpool tubs, had cookouts on the deck, and were hardly ever rushed or noisy. Jenna had never thought of them as houses that could have big trouble inside of them.

"There's nobody in there," Kate said, following Jenna's gaze.

"You mean they left you alone?" Jenna impatiently shook off her surprise and decided to store this knowledge for future use. Evidently *some* parents knew eleven-year-olds weren't babies.

"Oh, Jason's in there. He's supposed to be in charge, but we made this deal that he minds his business and I mind mine. He has to leave for his tennis lesson pretty soon, and then there'll really be nobody here unless Mom remembers and comes home. A lot of stuff slips her mind lately."

"It's okay if we stay outside." Jenna somehow felt Kate would be uncomfortable inside the house, but Kate showed no pleasure at her understanding. She merely shrugged and sat under a birch tree. Jenna joined her, and they fingered the curling white bark that peeled off like pencil shavings.

"So does this top-bunk deal have anything to do with your mom and the rules?" Kate prompted.

"Kind of. But, Kate, I need an adventure."

"Hmm. What kind of an adventure?"

"That's just it. I don't know what kinds of adventure there are! I need a *secret* adventure, Kate." Jenna deliberately lowered her voice. "This is *very* top bunk. Do you know what I mean? Did you ever—no, of course *you* didn't ever wish this, but . . ." Jenna sighed. "I might as well tell you. I mean, it's not as if you don't already know. Maybe you should know that I know so if I act stupid, you won't hold it against me."

"Jenna, what is it?" Kate whispered.

"I'm boring." Jenna's gaze slithered down to the grass, and she felt her cheeks glow hot.

"No, you're not boring!" Kate supplied, but her tone wasn't quite convincing.

"The thing is, everybody thinks they know all there is to know about me. It's like, if anyone asks if I've ever done something or gone somewhere, my parents can answer the question for me. 'Oh, yes, she had sushi once and spit it out,' or 'Oh, no, she's never been to Texas.' I want to be able to tell them stuff they don't already know. Do you know what I mean?" Jenna heard the little whine that was showing up at the end of her questions lately.

"Sure," said Kate. "And I've got an idea for an adventure. It just popped into my head since we're sitting out here looking at the neighborhood."

"Oh, I knew you would! But you would have gotten an idea inside your room, too."

"Sure," Kate said again and smiled. Something was missing in her smile, but her beautiful teeth showed. "Maybe a completely different idea in different surroundings. Is that a good adventurous thought?"

"Yes!" Jenna crowed, forgetting about using a top-bunk voice. "You mean we're maybe going on this adventure only because of where you were

63

when you thought it up? That sounds so—I can't think of the word. It means you don't plan things. Spontaneous!" she shouted. "Oh, Kate." Jenna scrambled to her feet. "I've hardly ever been spontaneous in my whole life. Except maybe when I mowed down Mrs. Geraldine Jarvis and her hurricane lamp!" She laughed recklessly. "What's the adventure?"

"How would you like to get your ears pierced?"

Surprise bloomed in her so completely that it blocked the words in her throat. "Are you kidding?" she finally managed. "But how can I do that? Lia has to get a parent's permission before any of the places at the mall will do it."

"You don't have to get it done at the mall," Kate said. "When my mom was a kid, your mom, too, most kids had it done by their friends. Jackie Peters lives right over there." Kate cocked her head toward a house across the street. "She learned how from her mom, and she's done about six people. That's her car there in the driveway, so she's home. If you want to go over and ask her, maybe she can do you today."

"While I'm here? Now?"

"Sure," Kate said. She studied Jenna and smiled with satisfaction. "You've got the perfect hair for it."

"Huh? What's hair got to do with it?"

Kate grasped the right side of Jenna's hair and

pulled it up. A few strands drifted back into place, but most of it stayed in the air. Next she pulled the hair forward and molded it against Jenna's jaw line. "Shake your head."

Jenna did.

"Your hair hardly moved. Unless your mom washes behind your ears or something, you can probably keep it hidden a long time. That way they find out when *you* want them to. Sound good?"

It sounded wonderful. It sounded like exactly what Jenna was looking for.

"Please, Jenna!" Kate grabbed her arm so suddenly that Jenna jumped. "Oh, please do this. It'll be so great!" Kate's eyes were shining. Her teeth were shining. All of Kate was shining at Jenna again.

Jenna smiled to think her wiry hair would finally be good for something.

❦

"If you hold the ice on there long enough, you won't feel a thing. Promise." Jackie, a skinny seventeen-year-old with oversize glasses, placed a needle, rubbing alcohol, and cotton balls on a tray. Her curly brown hair brushed her shoulders, its wildness controlled only by two thin gold barrettes not quite big enough to do the job. Her high-pitched voice seemed babyish to Jenna, but it was oddly comforting. Such a small, sweet, squeaky-voiced girl surely wouldn't cause tragedy to her earlobes.

Jenna relaxed, sure now that Jackie would go through with the ear-piercing. At first she had asked almost as many questions as Mom would, wanting to know if angry parents were going to come after her.

"Did you bring some earrings?" Jackie asked now.

"Earrings?"

"Yeah, I have to have something to stick through the holes." Jackie laughed. "But we've got millions of earrings here. I could let you have a pair." She rummaged in a dresser drawer that seemed to be stuffed with earring boxes. "Yeah, these are good. Fourteen-karat gold balls, real good quality. My mom bought these in the sixties for about three bucks. No charge."

Jenna gazed at the earring box, hardly daring to believe this girl would give her such a spectacular gift. Her stomach fizzed when Jackie actually lifted the hinged cover, the way it had when she'd walked all the way into Jackie's cheerfully tousled bedroom and sat down in her desk chair.

"Some people put a potato behind the ear for the needle to stick into when it comes out the other side," Jackie explained. "But I don't like the idea of potato juice getting in your ear when I pull the needle back through. You know?" Jackie wrinkled her nose. "So I'm going to use just a small piece of cardboard so the needle doesn't poke your neck."

Jenna nodded. Jackie sounded very competent. She had almost forgotten how cold her ears, upper jaw, and fingers were as she held the ice cubes to her lobes. Streams of water ran down her arms and her neck, which Kate mopped up every few minutes.

"Let's see how you're doing." Jackie walked over to Jenna's left shoulder and reached toward her ear. "Feel that?"

"Feel what?"

"Perfect. I pinched your earlobe with my fingernail. You didn't feel it?"

"Really? You really pinched me?"

Jackie smiled and began rubbing Jenna's earlobe with a cotton ball soaked in alcohol. Jenna couldn't feel this, but wisps of cotton tickled her cheek where the ice hadn't reached. "Now I'm going to use this Mercurochrome to make a tiny pink dot where I want to put the hole. This'll be over in no time."

Kate held the piece of cardboard behind Jenna's ear as Jackie worked, and Jenna heard the click as the needle came through her ear and met it. "Did you do it? Was that it?"

"Here comes the earring." Jackie plucked something off the tray and came back to her ear. "Great! Straight through. Fasten the back," Jackie pep-talked herself, "and there we have it." She straightened up. "You've got great ears, kid! Here, have a look in the mirror, but put ice on that right ear again for a couple minutes."

Jenna took the hand mirror that Jackie held out to her and looked at her left ear. She could hardly believe it. A gold ball sat right in the center of her lobe. Just like other people had! Just like Kate! She had thought it would never happen to her.

"This is really great, Jenna, just really, really great," Kate said.

"Right ear," Jackie coached herself. Jackie and Kate shifted to Jenna's right side. Again the rubbing, the dabbing, the cardboard, the click. "Kate, get some of those cotton balls to catch the blood," Jackie said.

"Blood?" asked Jenna.

"Well, my goodness," Jackie exclaimed like a shrill mother hen. "You're bleeding like a stuck pig here. I can't even see the hole."

For the first time it occurred to Jenna that getting her ears pierced someplace other than a doctor's office or jewelry store probably wasn't very safe.

"Don't let the blood drip on my top," Jenna begged.

"Here, we'll hold a bunch of tissues on it." Jackie reached into the box on a shelf near her bed and gave Jenna a handful. They made a scrunching sound near her ear like radio static. "There's no blood on your shirt. Now here. Look." She stretched her left arm all the way around Jenna's head and wiggled rubber-coated fingers in front of her face. "I do wear gloves, just so you know. And this needle has never stuck anybody before, and it never will again, 'cause I'll throw it away. Okay?"

Jenna nodded.

"Nevertheless, I think I'm going to stop piercing ears. It's just not as simple as it was in Mom's day. Lucky you, though." Jackie smiled. "Tonight I'm still in business." Her voice grew brisk as she took the tissues away. "Another alcohol rub, and then let's get an earring in there."

"Oh, Jenna this is just so great," Kate gushed.

"It's through!" Jackie exclaimed. "Here comes the back." Jenna heard the earring back click over the end of the post. "You're done!"

Jenna grabbed the mirror again. Now she had a gold ball centered in her right earlobe which exactly matched the left, but she was shocked at the size of her lobes. "They're pretty swollen, aren't they?" she said worriedly.

"That happens the first day," Jackie answered. "They'll look normal by tomorrow."

Jenna lowered the mirror and looked at Kate. "They're pierced. They're really pierced."

"You did it!" Kate said. "This is *so* great."

Jenna wondered fleetingly why Kate's vocabulary seemed so limited today. Usually she found new and snappy things to say without repeating herself. It was almost as if she had enjoyed the ear-piercing for her own reasons. But Jenna brushed the thoughts aside as she and Kate and Jackie exchanged thank-yous and you're-welcomes and good-byes. Jackie gave directions for turning the earrings in the holes to prevent sticking and for cleaning with alcohol twice a day for six weeks.

"Jenna, you did it. You really did it," Kate bub-bled, as they walked the short distance back to the Schmidts' house in the blue-gray light before sun-set. And then came the line Jenna actually hoped she wouldn't hear. "Oh, this is so great!"

"I'm really excited, too," Jenna said. "But why do you think it's so super great?"

"It's just—I just really feel right now like we're such good friends!" She linked arms with Jenna, her old zest returning. "Jenna, let's do something together. I've got another idea that'll help you with your secret life and be a lot of fun at the same time."

"Tonight? Won't your mom want us to stay in now?"

"Oh, it can't be tonight. We'll need a whole day. But I'm going to keep it a secret as a surprise for you. Okay?"

"Okay," Jenna agreed, "but how do you think up stuff?" Her little whine was back.

"Listen, Jenna, the important part of being mysterious," Kate whispered mysteriously, "isn't always the ideas you think up. *It's not telling every-thing you know."*

"Ooohhh." Jenna smoothed her hair around her ears.

"Now we could spend the rest of the night planning until your parents come and get you," Kate said as they arrived in her front yard. "But I'm not going to tell you how we're going to spend our adventure day until the day comes. So right now we'll have to do something else. Do the prayer meetings still get out as late as they used to?"

"Yeah, usually."

On this Wednesday night Kate's mom had agreed that Jenna could stay until her parents picked her up after prayer meeting. Jenna and Kate had first met at prayer meeting at the Jansens' sprawling, welcoming home way back when they were little girls.

"My parents haven't been going much lately," Kate said, as the girls watched Mrs. Schmidt move in front of the living room window and turn on a lamp. "My dad's too busy, and my mom doesn't want to go alone and have to explain where Dad is. But they go once in a while so people don't start calling them up and asking how they are."

"Oh." Jenna didn't know at all what to say.

"Everything's changing."

Jenna said nothing.

"So when your parents come," Kate said, "I

don't know if I want them to come in and talk to my mom or not. I kind of want them to, because I think if my parents are going to break up our family, they should have to explain to somebody who will tell them they shouldn't. And I kind of don't want them to, because my mom shouldn't be telling other people what's going on and not tell us, just because the other people are adults. If other people know my parents are getting a divorce before I know, I'm going to really be mad."

"Yeah," said Jenna.

"Anyway, let's think about the big day we're going to have. I don't know when we can do it, and I don't know all the details, but I'll call you up when it's time. I'll tell you what to wear and things like that, but other than that, just leave it up to me. Okay?" Kate turned to Jenna, and when Jenna looked, she was rewarded with Kate's wide smile. "Does that sound adventurous and mysterious to you?"

Jenna felt her own smile stretch and push out her cheeks. "Sounds fine." She was sure she knew what Kate would say next.

As dusk settled around them, Kate smiled even wider. "It's going to be really, really great."

❧ 7 ❧

Cans, Bees, and Quarters

*J*ENNA, I'M COMING, TOO."
Jenna almost fell off her bike as she turned to see Lia following her down the driveway. The frayed white threads of Lia's holey jeans pressed against her bare knee as she pedaled. When she pulled even, Jenna could see that she had rolled her hair behind her head, as if she'd taken in her sails, and tied it with a navy and white kerchief. The only hint of typical Lia was the apple-green and gold earrings that glinted in the middle of her earlobes. Lia had gotten her ears pierced after school.

"You really want to collect cans?" Jenna asked.

"Why should you get them all? You know I need money, too. When I get the dishwasher, you're going to benefit, aren't you?"

Jenna sighed. Never in their entire existence had Lia followed her before. Now she was doing it only to get something away from her.

"Honestly, Jenna, I'm a little hurt about your attitude. As Christians we should share, shouldn't we?"

"Well—maybe if you went to a different park, we'd get more total cans than we'll get if we go to the same place."

"Oh no," Lia objected as they turned from Nicolet Street south onto Lincoln. Here they had to ride single file in the bike lane, with the noise of heavier traffic. For the second time in their lives Lia followed her, for the purpose of shouting in her ear. "I heard what David told you about summer league baseball getting started and that you'd find tons of cans under the bleachers at the ball park the day after a game. Of course, not that I needed David to tell me that."

At least riding in front, Jenna could be excused for ignoring Lia. She turned left on Wisconsin Avenue with the green light, which was always kind of scary even though she knew the traffic was supposed to hold still for her. Now the breeze blew at her left side, rustling the plastic garbage bag she carried in her bike basket, pushing at the empty backpack that lay shrunken against her shoulder blades like a molting skin. With one victorious gust, as she wove around the rear bumpers of the parked cars, the wind uncovered her left ear.

Frantically she tried to scoop her hair back in place as she sailed down the bridge, past the high school, on to the ball park. When she stopped her bike, her hair would be in stiff huge swirls, as if she were wearing the darkest rain cloud in history on her head, and her gold ball earrings would stick right out for Lia to see. Maybe she should duck into the restroom before Lia could catch up. If only she had a comb!

No time. She raked hair over her ears as best she could and scrambled under the bleachers, pushing cans into her garbage bag. It began to bulge.

"See, there's plenty for both of us." Lia's bag was getting full, too. "But they're awfully sticky."

Aha, thought Jenna, *Lia the Lovely is too dainty for this job.*

"Cans that are supposed to be empty sure have a lot of liquid left in them."

Jenna crowded more cans into her bag.

"This is a boring way to make money."

"Are you kidding?" Jenna tied her bag shut with a twist tie. "They're just laying here for you to pick up. How easy can it get? I'm going to look in the dumpster."

"Yuck!"

The top edge of the dumpster was high off the ground for Jenna. She balanced on her stomach to lean inside, her feet dangling above the ground, the wood digging into her ribs. She closed her eyes on the half-eaten hot dogs and ketchup-smeared napkins and greasy popcorn bags as much as she could and plucked out cans. Flies tickled her.

"Uh—Jenna?" Lia's voice floated above her. "Since that doesn't seem to bother you, would you mind filling up this other bag a little more? It *is* for the dishwasher, and you will get to use it—"

Jenna came out of the dumpster. "You don't think I mind garbage?"

"Well, you do get right in there."

"Aren't you the one who's saving for the dishwasher?"

"Well, yes, but others will get to use it, and after all, I had the idea, and I'll take the risk of actually buying it. I mean, the idea itself is the biggest contribution, wouldn't you say?"

"You think you can stand there all cool and calm—"

"Hey, I'm plenty sticky, too. Don't get mad now 'cause I wanted to tell you how I admire your Christian growth. I really mean it. I think this is just what the Bible means when it talks about being humble and working hard with your hands—"

Anger boiled from Jenna's stomach to her mouth as if she were a volcano. "You just think you're so important! You think I'm so simple and boring and low that I should dig around in there with flies and bees and ants and roaches. Probably rats eat supper here."

"Jenna, you're spoiling—"

Fresh anger seized her. "You think I'm so dull and boring I'll keep your dishwasher secret even if you treat me however you want. I could blow your stupid secret, you know." Jenna hated saying this even as the words came from her mouth.

"I could tell on you unless you do things my way. Did you ever think of that?" Her voice had lost its power. Jenna Vander Giffin was a holder of secrets, not a spiller of them, and now something twisted and uprooted inside her.

They eyed each other carefully, still grasping their clanking bags of cans. Jenna's gooey, lumpy backpack smelled like beer.

"You won't tell." Lia did not smirk. She looked almost plain.

So Lia knew her, too. Wasn't she even worried? She should have enough humility to worry. Jenna jammed her kickstand up and pedaled out of the ball park. But she didn't want Lia to worry about her secret. She lowered her head and drove her pedals faster, against the wind now, downshifting her gears. So often she had wanted Lia to trust her, to notice her. Lia finally had. Jenna didn't want Lia to feel she'd made a mistake.

"Get your bag up more," Lia's voice came behind her. "You'll wear a hole in it and lose half your cans on the road."

Lia's bagful was probably small enough to balance across her basket. Jenna tried to hoist hers while steering with one hand, but she couldn't keep the bag from dragging. Finally she pulled it partway onto her leg where it got in the way of her pedaling.

A crushed can pierced the bag and scraped her knee. Fortunately by this time they pulled into the gravel lot where the recycling machine stood. The machine was called the Golden Goat.

"Bees," moaned Lia.

Jenna whopped hair over her ears, flinched as her hair stuck to her hands, and approached the Goat. She hated bees, too, but it was either stuff these cans in the metal monster or run away and admit she'd gotten sticky and tired and quarrelsome for nothing. It was either earn some money and get closer to putting Mrs. Geraldine Jarvis and her hurricane lamp behind her, or run away and lose a chance to be braver than Lia. She wrenched open her bag and began to choke the Golden Goat with aluminum.

Bees hummed their threatening tones as their wings fanned her arms. They buzzed in a wicked chorus around her hair, which felt like cotton candy. She jammed the machine too full and had to wait agonizing seconds for it to eat the cans and get ready for more. Something slightly furry settled on her jaw and walked toward her ear.

"A bee!" Lia cried in operatic soprano. "I'll brush it off you. If I can find a Kleenex or something—"

Jenna dropped her cans with a clatter and

scooped the bee away. She beat hair over her earrings. A car filled with kids and a father drove up.

"Are they getting in your hair?" Lia sang.

Quarters began to clank into the coin return.

"Here!" Lia began to flick a cloth about Jenna's
head. Darting like a snake's tongue, it licked a
large tuft of hair from the side of her face, straight
back.

Jenna screamed.

Quarters clanked faster, like popcorn.

"Did you get stung?"

"You girls okay?" The man in the car spoke
with the slightest shade of a chuckle.

"Hey, girlie, your money's fallin' all over the
ground," came a boy's hoarse voice.

Jenna swiped hair over her ears, and her cheeks
for good measure, and then dropped down to the
stones to retrieve her quarters.

"Let me see the sting," Lia insisted.

"No sting!" Jenna shouted. The only thing
worse than having a bee dive under her hair and
sting her pierced ears would be Lia warbling all
the way up the scale about Jenna's hidden plain
gold balls, when her own earrings were delicate
spring green and she could tie her hair back.

Overhead the quarters slowed—clang, clink.

*C'mon, give me a couple more. Spit me out another
one*, Jenna found herself begging silently. Sorting
quarters from the gravel to stuff into her backpack,

pitching her dropped cans down the Goat's throat, she resisted the urge to roll in the stones to ward off the bees.

A pleasant male voice interrupted her thoughts. "Can I help with your cans?"

Jenna looked up sharply. A teenage boy from the car stood over her. But he wasn't looking down. He was looking—at Lia whose golden hair now tumbled around her shoulders. The navy and white scarf, which she had used to beat the bees off, now dangled from her hand, switching against Jenna's nose.

"Oh, thank you. That would be great." Lia's prettiest musical tones emerged from her smiling mouth as she handed her neatly tied bag across Jenna's body.

Jenna crawled out of the way. It didn't occur to her till much later that she wouldn't have had to wait.

"It feels good to have the money at the end, doesn't it?" Lia came to the edge of the lot where Jenna stood with the bikes, cupping quarters in a fine-boned hand, still smiling gloriously.

Only the money? Jenna thought.

"Can I put my money in one of the compartments in your backpack?"

Jenna nodded tiredly.

"You have more than I do." Lia spoke from

behind her as Jenna felt the small tuggings at the pack on her back.

"More *what?*" Jenna asked.

"Money, dummy. You know, we didn't get all the cans at the ball park. I think I'm going back." Lia swung her leg over her bike.

No way. No way did Jenna want to go back—but no way was Lia going to come out of this with as much or more money than she had on top of everything else. Jenna looked morosely at the tattered garbage bag stuffed in her basket and at the neater and probably cleaner one in Lia's.

"You know, I did get stung over there," said Lia.

Jenna raised a questioning face to her sister, and Lia nodded. "Matt brushed it off, but it got me."

"Where," asked Jenna. "Where did you get stung?"

"On the shoulder."

Jenna nodded. It was a pretty place to get stung. Not like a nose or a lip—or a big fat eyebrow.

"So I'm game if you are. Coming? I'll race you." Nimbly, Lia took off.

You're on. Jenna slapped her feet on the pedals, squeezed the hand grips, and followed Lia down the road. Too late, she murmured, "I'm coming, too."

❧ 8 ❧

Life Books

"ENNA!" THE HARSH WHISPER PENE-
trated the sleep just beginning to veil her.
"Jenna!"

Across the dark bedroom, a small flashlight
switched on. Sherry slipped out of her bed and
crouched on all fours next to Jenna's. "I want to
show you my Life Book."

Glancing toward the other end of the room
where Maria slept, Jenna dropped on her knees to
the carpet. Casually, she raked her fingers through
her hair to form tents over her ears, glad she
remembered so soon after waking to hide her earrings. She resisted the temptation to scratch her
lobes. Jenna had been faithfully twirling the earrings in their holes as if winding a tiny toy, and
she'd been faithfully applying alcohol with cotton
balls, cotton swabs, and an eyedropper, but her
ears had begun to itch. She hoped it didn't mean
anything.

Sherry's Life Book was a yellow photo album with drawings and papers sealed under its plastic-coated pages. "Laurie's working on it with me. She wants me to make a record of my whole life."

"Kind of like our baby books," Jenna said. "Mom keeps them in the attic." *Kind of like my journal, too*, Jenna thought, because she hid her journal away just as Sherry hid her Life Book. But she hadn't gotten her journal out in a while. The thought ran through her mind that her journal was mostly prayers, and she let the thought run right on through.

Sherry sat up tall. "I don't need a baby book, whatever that is. It's a *Life* Book."

"Moms write baby facts about you in baby books. But people still put stuff in them after you're a baby," Jenna added hurriedly, not wanting Sherry to be offended. "Hey, maybe they should call them Growing Up Books or something. No, wait. They *should* call them Life Books." Jenna began to feel excited. "When you're a kid, that's life, right? Sherry, did Laurie make up the name Life Book?"

Sherry shrugged.

"'Cause if she did, then I like her even better than I do already."

"Some of the stuff Laurie put in for me. Look at this." Sherry turned to a page near the front which held a pink-edged chart of birth facts. In the small weak circle of the flashlight, Jenna read:

Mother: Christine Ann Johnson.

"Her whole name," Sherry said reverently.

Jenna sat quietly, knowing Sherry was thinking about her mother who'd disappeared three years ago.

"And that's *really* her whole name," Sherry stressed, still whispering. "Laurie said. So I'm really Sherry Johnson."

Jenna's eyes drifted to the blank line on the pink-edged card, patiently stretching out after the word *Father:* Those two dots, the colon, were like a prompt for information, and they'd been sitting on that card prompting for eleven whole years without getting a response. Even though no one knew what to write on the father line of Sherry's card, Jenna felt glad that Sherry could be sure of her own name at last.

"My mom and I did fun things," Sherry murmured. "We used to drink green Kool-Aid out of teacups, an' we used to jump on the couch, and lay in bed real late at night and watch scary movies and pull the covers over our heads. And we used to go downstairs and sit in the tavern and dance with her friends." Sherry paused. "People used to talk about her and say she was no good."

Jenna was quiet for a moment. "Let's see what

else it says," she encouraged. "You were born in Green Bay at St. Vincent Hospital."

"I was pretty sure it was Green Bay."

"Four pounds, twelve ounces!"

"What's the matter with that?"

"Skinny is what's the matter with that. All the babies my mom had weighed seven or eight pounds. But, Sherry, this is really great that Laurie is doing this with you. This is part of your secret side."

"My what?" Sherry whispered.

"A part of you that people don't know about. This stuff was such a secret side it was even secret from you. I don't like that. I don't like when adults know stuff about you that you don't even know yourself."

"Yeah," said Sherry.

"I raised money by myself tonight to pay for Mrs. Jarvis and her you-know-what. Mom and Dad knew I was doing it, but I did it myself."

"How did you get money?"

Jenna told the story of the aluminum cans. She left Lia out to protect her secret, but even more she left Lia out because Lia had nothing to do with the hurricane lamp. Jenna *had* done it herself.

"And I stuffed the quarters in my backpack—oh no!" Jenna suddenly interrupted herself in a whisper that had too much voice mixed in.

"What?"

"I forgot to ask Mom if you can put backpacks in the washer. It's all sticky inside from pop, and it stinks like beer and I need it tomorrow! Oh, well, I guess I just can't take it." Suddenly it seemed funny. She laughed—too loudly. "Not when Mom smells it, I won't be able to!"

Across the room Maria sighed, turned over, and churned her arms and legs all over her bed looking for a comfortable position.

"We better stop this," Sherry whispered. "You better go back to bed now so you're not too tired in the morning."

"Yeah," Jenna said. "But you have to, too."

"Oh, I will. I just want to look at my Life Book for a couple minutes longer. Maybe being alone in the dark when it's quiet will help me remember more stuff about my childhood. Laurie wants me to do that. You can think good when you're alone, right, Jenna?"

"Uh-huh," Jenna said. She climbed back into bed, but she was suddenly feeling uneasy, as though Sherry was up to something she was willing to hint at but not tell. Why did it always seem that people reminded her of her love for privacy when they had a scheme up their sleeve? On the other hand, how could she, who did love her privacy, begrudge other people theirs?

Thinking of Sherry's Life Book, Jenna reached down between her bed and the wall for her journal, the pretty book covered with flowered cloth that she'd gotten for her last birthday. She couldn't read it in the dark, but she'd written in the dark before.

Yes, there was a pen down there, too, resting in the low spot between the carpet and the baseboard. Wriggling her fingers like a spider, she worked it loose and grasped it.

Dear Jesus,

She didn't know what to write. Even in the dark, her greeting and its comma prompted her just like that *Father:* line in Sherry's Life Book.

You know about the cans.

Of course He did. Boring.

*I'm boring. Everybody thinks they own me.
I'm going to find a secret side and keep it all to
myself.*

She didn't know what to put next. She felt empty of things to say to the Lord. There should be something she could write now, something secret, something no one could possibly know because it was new under the sun.

King Solomon in the Bible had said nothing was new under the sun. Once she'd asked Dad what that meant, and he said it meant that all of the things that were done or said or thought on earth—"under the sun"—had been done or said or thought before by countless people who had lived and died ages ago. Jenna wasn't so sure she understood that. When the Wright brothers had flown the first airplane, no one had done that before, had they? Somebody had to be the first person to use a computer, didn't they? Of course, maybe they were just doing the same traveling or the same work people had done before, only in newer, faster ways. And of course by now lots of people had been born and died who had flown in airplanes or used computers. Still Jenna thought she should be able to write something down that was totally hers, totally new—new under the sun.

A strange feeling washed over her, so strong she closed her journal. It didn't seem safe to defy King Solomon. Squirming, she dropped the book and pen back down between her bed and the wall with a muffled thump. It was too dark to read what she'd written to the Lord anyway. He knew what she'd said. Maybe she could just pray a little now. *Jesus*, she managed to call inwardly. But whatever she'd meant to say to Him melted away as she fell asleep.

9

Sherry's Scheme

JENNA JUMPED AND HER ARMS JACK-
knifed, her elbow cracking painfully as her
alarm clock sputtered to life. She went limp and
groaned. Boy, that short time spent talking last
night must have taken a big bite out of her sleep.
She forced her eyes open and groped for the shut-
off button. Stupid, hoarse, ancient clock that Dad
had taken to college. Couldn't she get a nice digi-
tal clock radio with two wake-up settings and a
snooze bar? Why should the first sound that
entered her head every day be this cross between
a jackhammer and a clothes dryer filled with
rocks?

"Good morning, Jenna," Maria chirped. Maria
always awakened bright and cheerful, and she had
a whole "Good morning" litany that reminded
Jenna of the careful way Ben pronounced his
words.

"I guess you haven't memorized the verse about not waking your friend with a loud greeting."

"I'm not being loud," Maria chirped. "And waking you up is the clock's fault. Good morning, Sherry."

For the first time Jenna looked at Sherry, and gasped.

She was sprawled on top of the covers, hair scattered like corn silk, as if she had barely managed to make it onto the bed in the act of passing out from total exhaustion. She was deeply asleep. Her Life Book was pushed only partway under her bed, and the flashlight shone a feeble amber patch on the carpet.

Maria padded over to Sherry's bedside. "Good morning, Sherry. What's this?" She bent down and pulled at the Life Book.

"That's Sherry's personal stuff. Just leave it, okay?"

"Life Book," Maria said. "See, I can read. What's a Life Book?"

"It's like a—" No. She wasn't going to say baby book.

"Sherry." Maria straightened. "Get up. If you're late for school, you'll get marked retarded."

"Maria!" Jenna burst out laughing. "That's tardy." She quickly grew serious when she saw their noise had no effect on Sherry. "Sherry. Sherry. Wake up."

Sherry rolled over and scrubbed hair out of her face. "Wha—? Jenna?"

"It's time for school," Jenna urged. "If you've got a breakfast chore, you'd better hurry!"

"School? Uh—oh no. Too tired." She rolled face down again.

"Sherry! How late did you sit up last night?"

Sherry only moaned.

"She sat up late last night?" Maria said. "Reading her Life Book?"

"We'd better get going. Why don't you go first and see if the bathroom's free? I'll start getting dressed." Jenna dragged jeans and her newest T-shirt from the closet. "Sherry, what's going on?" She asked as soon as Maria left.

Sherry snored.

"You're faking!"

"I'm not going to school," Sherry said in a far-away voice. "I'm too tired. Sometimes Mom and Dad—your mom and dad—don't go places 'cause they're too tired. So I'm not going to school. I'm too tired."

"You sat up late on purpose, didn't you? I mean, so this would happen."

Sherry yawned and stretched elaborately.

"You sat up late on purpose?" Maria came in and closed the door behind her.

There was a knock.

"You may come in, Mom," Maria said. "Know how I knew it was Mom? I saw her coming. Good morning, Mom."

"Morning, hon. Sherry, are you ill?" Mom

crossed the room to Sherry's bed. Her toe kicked the flashlight, and she looked down.

"She stayed up all night on purpose for an accident," Maria said.

"What?" Mom looked at Maria, then back to Sherry, and laid her palm on Sherry's forehead. "She doesn't feel feverish. Now what's this about staying up all night?"

"It wasn't *all night*, Maria," Jenna exclaimed and then realized her mistake as Mom turned to her. "I mean, it couldn't have been. She got in bed the same time I did, and I'm sure she fell asleep first."

"She told you then this morning that she'd been up during the night?"

"No, Jenna already knew," Maria said. "She asked her how late she stayed up. Sherry didn't say anything about it."

"So you were up too, Jenna?" Mom looked down again at the flashlight. "What's this? This looks like a note for you."

A piece of torn notebook paper lay on the floor. It hadn't been there a moment before, and Jenna thought it must have fluttered down from her bed or night table or dresser. Her name was scrawled at the top in Sherry's handwriting.

"Your backpack's in the dryer," the note read.

"Why did you stick—Sherry! You mean you washed my backpack in the middle of the night?"

"Why did you do that, Sherry?" Mom asked. She didn't use her scolding voice. It was a really-wanting-to-know voice. Mom probably couldn't figure out if Sherry had gone back to pleasing everyone or if there was rebellion in there somewhere.

"Well, I told her how it got all gunky from the cans—," Jenna began.

"Did you make her feel somehow that she should do this—"

"It's not her fault." Sherry's suddenly clear voice made Jenna jump. "She got up 'cause I needed her, and she went back to bed. I'm not going to school 'cause I'm too tired." She pushed her hands up under her pillow and gripped the edge of the mattress.

"Oh, so this is a challenge," Mom said softly. "'On purpose for an accident' means you purposely got no rest so you'd honestly not be able to get up for school. Sherry, you're wondering if we'll decide you're too naughty to be a Vander Giffin, aren't you?"

Jenna looked at Mom in amazement.

"Hey? Is there any breakfast today?" David's voice in the hall seemed to speak to no one in particular. "I'm starving."

"What's the drama going on in here?" Lia asked, coming into the room.

"Sherry wants to be too naughty to be a Vander

Giffin," Maria said in a tone of complete confusion.

"Ha-ha-ha, if you can be too naughty, Mom 'n' Dad'll have to kick out half the family." Peter was standing in the doorway.

Lia raised her eyebrows and leaned her head toward Jenna's, hair falling forward like a curtain to hide her mouth. "I guess this'll challenge the ol' parenting skills, huh?" she whispered. "Sherry," she said aloud, straightening up. "It seems to me Peter's right. If a person could be too naughty to live here, this family would be a whole lot smaller. So how about if you just get up and come with us to breakfast?"

Sherry didn't move.

"Make her, Mom," Peter said.

Sherry curled her hands over the edge of the mattress and tried to stuff them under.

"Okay, everybody, let's get down to breakfast," Mom said. "Or you'll all be late. Sherry, we want you to join us. If you choose not to, you'll face the consequences of being late for school, just like anyone else in the family." She turned and left the room.

"I'll be down in a minute, Mom," Lia sang. "I just have to clean my ears."

"Lia, that sounds so gross." Cara's footsteps clumped past the room and down the steps. Cara had begun jabbing and digging at Lia in little ways.

Jenna, who had taken two giant steps forward with the intention of dashing to the bathroom to wipe her own earlobes with alcohol, stopped dead. She decided to dash to the basement instead and find out if her backpack had survived the washer and dryer. She found it wound up in its own straps and dangling a few raveled threads. Tearing up the basement stairs while trying to unscramble the pack, she found the downstairs bathroom free. Her secret stash of alcohol and cotton balls was, of course, upstairs in her room.

"Jenna, *there* you are." Mom sounded a bit exasperated. "I want you to take Sherry's turn at pouring juice."

"Bathroom!" Jenna cried, charging through the dining room, heading for the stairs. As fast as she could, she drizzled alcohol under and around her earrings, spun them in their holes, swiped at her streaming neck with a towel, combed an earmuff of hair over each ear, and galloped back down the stairs. The wind she created barely stirred her hair. To think that in some ways her dark, bristly hair was better than the blonde, silken, flowing locks of Lia!

Jenna tried to settle down at the table, but breakfast continued to be hurried and noisy. The oatmeal had been reheated in the microwave, and it reminded Jenna of wallpaper paste. Mom and Dad spent most of the meal talking in the den, and the part Jenna overheard was about Sherry's Life Book. Maybe the book wasn't so good for her, they were saying. They understood that Laurie meant to help Sherry with questions about her past, but maybe the book made her dwell on her early childhood and her birth mother too much. Maybe it enticed her to feel dissatisfied with the family.

"Don't worry, Jenna," Maria whispered, as Jenna zipped her jacket and looked uncertainly toward the stairs. "I'll help Mom take care of her, and I'll teach Ben and Tyler how, so when I go to school this afternoon they'll know what to do."

Thinking that maybe no one knew what to do, Jenna smiled anyway. "Thanks."

"Do you think she's gonna get disbanded from school?"

"You mean suspended?"

"Nah," David said, slinging his book bag over his shoulder and heading out the back door. "That's only for fighting or smoking or carrying a weapon or stuff."

"A weapon?" Maria shrieked.

Ben bit a slice of bread into the shape of a gun and began shooting with it: "Hehehehehehehe-heheheh!"

"Make my day, kid." Cara was gone.

"Honestly, can you imagine getting suspended for skipping school? Sounds like some nonsensical rule the schools would think up." Lia went out the door. Her hair fell alluringly to one side, exposing one ear and its earring.

"But if she doesn't go to school, Mom and Dad can get put in jail!" Peter pulled on his backpack and ran out.

"Is that true? Can they go to jail for real?" Maria asked.

"They would make her—"

"Owie! Mow-ee-ah! Bump-ped head," Tyler cried.

"I gotta run." Jenna let the outer door fall shut with its familiar *clop*. Life alone with Mom in the morning, with Maria, Ben, and Tyler, with Sherry stubbornly in bed, was something unknown to her. Maybe it was like a secret side, but it was one that didn't tempt her. Her family, sounding so normal, had run on ahead, and she followed them down the faithful, unchanging concrete path to school.

❧ 10 ❧

Empty Chairs

FRIDAY, JUNE 5, WAS THE LAST HALF-day of school. That afternoon Jenna took three layers of cake that she had baked for the family's Annual School's-Out Cookout from the freezer. She set them, chocolate, orange, and spice, on the counter next to the huge bowl of white frosting, tubes of green decorating frosting, waxed paper, toothpicks, cardboard circles, and a cake plate. Now she was ready to put the whole thing together into a triple-decker delight piped with a trellis design and decorated with frosting leaves and fresh flowers.

The cake in the picture was a work of art. Jenna frowned at it. Mom was going to pay her five dollars toward Mrs. Geraldine Jarvis and her hurricane lamp if only she could reproduce this masterpiece and save Mom the trouble of baking a cake herself, or paying twice as much money for half as much cake at the store. Baking was one thing—she just followed a recipe, and everything turned out flaky or moist or smooth or chewy or however it was supposed to be. But cake decorating, she realized too late, was art. And at art she was dismal.

People streamed in and out in their shorts and T-shirts, clutching bats, balls and mitts, jacks and jump ropes, and in Ben's case an old purse stuffed with stones and weeds. Jenna carefully unwrapped the cake layers and began slicing their rounded tops flat.

Picking up the frosting knife, she piled two scoops of creamy white frosting onto her smallest layer. As she began swirling it over the top and sides, she wished she could rub her earlobes. They felt raw and gummy. She was about to set the knife down and sneak her fingers under her hair when Mom came through the back door.

"Hi, hon. See what I got from Mrs. Schubert's garden? These flowers are actually safe to eat! They match the picture pretty well, don't they?" Mom held a small bunch of pink, white, yellow, and purple blossoms up to the page. "Some of these can go on the edge of the cake plate, some can go here and there on your trellis design, and with a twist tie we can put together a little nosegay for the top."

"Thanks, Mom," Jenna managed. Mom had already asked her if she'd like to take a cake-decorating class. She'd already helped her rearrange the refrigerator to make room for the frosted cake layers. Now she was forming a perfect nosegay for the top of her cake, poking the flowers to arrange them just so, and even covering the twist tie with yellow ribbon. But Jenna's pierced ears—the secret she had kept from Mom—were infected, and she was sure that if Mom did one more nice thing, she was going to get really grumpy.

Jenna breathed a sigh of relief as Mom left the kitchen. She tucked the nosegay into the refrigerator, slid the frosted layer on its cardboard base carefully onto the middle shelf, and went to work frosting the orange layer.

She had faithfully cleaned her earlobes twice a day in the two and a half weeks since they'd been pierced. She had regularly twisted the posts around and around in their little tunnels, sometimes in the bathroom and sometimes, when she needed to hide, in the closet or even the attic. She felt this diligent care was quite an accomplishment for someone who lived in as public a house as she did. But was she rewarded for all this responsibility by nicely healing ears that would be ready for new, prettier earrings in four weeks? She was not!

Jenna put the orange layer in the refrigerator and began to frost the large chocolate layer.

Both plain gold balls had margins of red around

them, and if she pinched a little bit, some thick whitish stuff oozed out. This morning she had bravely squeezed all the gunk out, and bathed, rinsed, and showered her ears in alcohol. If she could have taken her ears off and left them behind to soak in a cup on the bathroom counter, like dentures, she would have. She could hardly bear to admit it, but she thought she probably had to start her six weeks of healing over again.

Jenna took her smallest frosted layer, the spice cake, from the refrigerator. The frosting was set, so she began poking a toothpick around its edge, where the numbers on a clock would be, to mark the pattern for the trellis design.

She might have worked up the courage to call Jackie and ask what to do about her ears, but she couldn't remember Jackie's last name. Kate could help by giving her both the information she needed and the courage, but where was Kate these days? She hadn't said a word about their Secret Side Day. Jenna had called her twice. Once she hadn't been home, and the other time she'd said she was in a hurry—she had to go somewhere, it was the wrong time, she'd call when she could.

"Did you think about our adventure?" Jenna had asked. "Do you need to think about it, or does the whole plan come at once?" *Do you just reach into your secret side and pull ideas out?* she wanted to ask. *Things to say?*

"Jen-naah." Kate's voice trailed off tiredly.

"Can I sleep over?" She could soothe that frustration out of Kate. She could stick right with Kate, first thing in the morning, last thing at night. She could solve Kate, see how she worked.

"Aw—no." Kate was almost pleading. "Things are so up in the air around here."

"But it's only me. I don't care." *You don't have to hide it from me. Don't go more secret on me than you already are.*

"I gotta go." Click.

Jenna piped the edges of her cake layers with thick green lines of frosting. If Kate was going to fold more and more inside herself, Jenna fretted, how could her own secret life get off the ground? She sighed. She was just plain boring Jenna with her wings clipped until Kate Schmidt got good and ready to teach her to fly.

Her hand jerked as she drew her last ribbon of trellis, breaking the green line. She poked it together with a knife, lifted the center tier on its cardboard base, and placed it carefully in the middle of the bottom layer. The trellis lines matched!

Jenna straightened up and purposely smoothed the frown off her forehead. *Thank you, Lord*, she thought, pleased. She positioned the top layer, drew green frosting leaves all over the trellis design, and stepped back.

"Wow."

Jenna jumped. Lia stood in the doorway. "Fresh flowers come later. Just before we eat it."

"It's gorgeous," Lia said.

"I could use your dishwasher right about now," Jenna whispered, cocking her head toward the sink overflowing with all the pots she'd used or accidently smeared with frosting. The cake had improved her mood, and Lia was, of course, another person who knew how to have a secret life.

"Oh, that." Lia sniffed.

"Aren't you going to get the dishwasher?"

Lia lifted her nose and shrugged. "Maybe. Maybe not. I might spend my money on other things."

Jenna suspected the dishwasher money wasn't mounting up as fast as Lia wanted. Lia did babysit though. Maybe she wanted to spend her money on personal things instead. Jenna thought of the tubes of paints and drawing pencils and inks Lia had bought recently.

"You know Sherry's getting away with murder, don't you?"

"Well . . ." It was true Sherry had done a lot of things Jenna would never have dared. Jenna had never stayed out late or skipped school or refused to do homework because she couldn't imagine living to tell about it. Yet here was Sherry, alive on the other side of disobedience. It was enough to make a person angry.

"Where is Sherry anyway?" Jenna asked.

Lia shrugged, and Jenna noticed fleetingly how graceful even Lia's shrugs were. "Haven't seen her since lunch."

Lunch. That was when Sherry'd handed Mom her report card full of failures and incompletes, with a note attached saying she'd done no work the last three weeks. Her promotion to sixth grade was conditional.

"I'm so disappointed in this, Sherry," Mom had said. "You'll have to go to summer school to catch up."

"I guess I'm just no good," Sherry had answered.

And then the family had sat down to lunch, and Sherry had excused herself a split second before Dad began the prayer.

"I'm not sure I'm a Christian," she had explained mildly from the foot of the stairs. "No, I don't think I am. I hope you don't mind too much."

"Then I think," Dad said carefully, "you can still remain seated and be respectfully quiet during the prayer. And if you want to talk about this later—fine."

But, thin-lipped and round-eyed, Sherry had

shaken her head and refused both prayer and lunch. No one had even gone upstairs after her.

"Did you ever even *think* of pulling something like Sherry did at lunch today?" Lia's hushed voice, lingering over each word, broke Jenna's thoughts.

Jenna didn't need to answer.

"Well, I'll tell you the sincere, honest truth," Lia hissed. "Neither did I." She paused, head still inclined toward Jenna, hair masking her profile, one earring twinkling. "And I can't wear *makeup?*" Lia let that sink in, then turned on her heel, and went upstairs.

❦

The dining room table was dressed in a checkered cloth. Buttered buns towered over rims of baskets; crisp sliced pickles and sweet onions scented the air. Vegetable plates and fruit salad made a kaleidoscope of color, and plump brats and hamburgers rode proudly on platters carried in from the grill. Jenna's eyes closed, and her mouth watered at their meaty smell.

"Places, everybody."

The dive for the table reminded Jenna of musical chairs, but when everyone was seated, two places were empty.

"What is this?" Dad said. "Are we disappearing one by one here, or what?"

"There were ten in the bed, and the little one sa-ai-id-d," Cara sang, "I'm crowded. Roll o-ver. So they all rolled over, and one fell out—"

"Cara!"

"Well, nobody cares if Lia sings. She gets to sing any old time she wants, and everybody thinks she's wonderful—"

"Ha-ha, that's *wunderbar*."

"Eleven!" Jenna shouted above the fray. "There's eleven in our bed."

"What're you yammering about? Can we eat?" complained David. "I got a baseball game after supper, in case anybody remembers."

You forgot Sherry! Jenna wanted to yell, but she didn't because Sherry might be in the house. Didn't they know that being forgotten, that not belonging, was just what Sherry was afraid of?

"I am double triple starving," Ben said. "Let us pray."

"Yes," Mom broke in with feeling. "Let us pray."

It would be more than a meal prayer, Jenna knew instantly, and for some reason that knowledge was uncomfortable. Mom began praying for Sherry's safety, for Sherry to know how loved she was.

Jenna tried to join in, in her heart, because she, too, wanted Sherry to be safe and to know she was loved. But something was stopping her. She felt as if her brain had toughened up like rubber, and the words just bounced around inside and never reached God's ears. Everyone was making all this fuss over poor, fragile Sherry and leaving all this space for winsome, artistic Lia. Drab, tame Jenna was just expected to be here, praying and eating a plain hamburger on an unbuttered bun with maybe one wild dollop of red ketchup.

When Mom's prayer faltered, Dad took over, asking God in a fervent voice to help them establish a secure home for Sherry, to help them be fair with all of the children, to give them wisdom to guide the family.

Jenna's heart wanted to melt around the edges, but she stiffened in her chair. The veins in her temples ached.

"Sherry wants us to come after her," Mom said.

"Yes," Jenna agreed, and all eyes turned to her.

"Did she tell you she was going, Jenna?" Mom's voice was a plea for honesty, vulnerable but dignified. For a moment Jenna felt more grown up, less angry, yet Mom didn't seem to believe she could just know how Sherry felt.

"Do you know where we should look?" Dad asked.

Jenna watched Dad's face for several seconds, but his question, his preoccupation with Sherry, stayed. She looked away slowly, looked down at her dreary burger, but didn't dare not answer. She shook her head, her spirits sinking even lower because she had done so. She changed the subject.

"Lia will come back while you're gone. She'll be wearing makeup. If you're not here, she'll be madder than ever."

"How do you know that?" Cara asked.

Jenna met Cara's blue eyes, which were wide and, Jenna thought, betrayed. "She just will." She turned her look on Mom, who contemplated her for a long moment.

"I'll stay," Mom said rather explosively, running a hand over her hair. This seemed to be an admission that the rest of the family was about to launch a search for Sherry. "I'll let Lia skip supper and face me in her makeup."

Mom was not waiting to get her hands on Lia, Jenna thought. For Lia Mom was making some kind of loving sacrifice, some bending of the rule. Yet Mom had just believed her, Jenna, without question. She felt the mix of resentment and relief again.

Dad wiped his mouth with his napkin and pushed away from the table. "Jenna, if you have any idea where Sherry might be, now's the time."

Why am I responsible to know, Jenna wished she could say, but Maria interrupted her mental protest.

"I bet she's looking up her life! Like she did that one night in her Lifesaver Book. Do adopted kids always get that? I mean, a book where they can look up their whole life?"

Mom and Dad exchanged significant looks. The meal, Jenna suddenly knew, was over.

"I'll put the meat in the fridge." David shoved the last of his hamburger into his mouth, and Jenna knew he was being so generous to help because *he* had already eaten.

"I'm going after Sherry," said Dad.

"I should be going with you." Mom sighed. "Oh, Lord, there's only one of me."

"He knows, Lin." Dad paused before jumping up from the table. "He'll go with all of us."

"I want to go get Sherry, too!" declared Maria.

"I wanna see Lia," Cara chimed in. "I bet she'll be beautiful."

One by one, the family members pushed food into the refrigerator, dishes into the sink, and scattered. A few went with Dad to gather Sherry in, a few stayed with Mom to be part of Lia's audience, a few went in directions of their own. As Jenna entered the kitchen, the cake waiting on the table, trimmed in its fresh flowers, caught her eye. It looked like a wedding cake, sweet and romantic. But what she'd built would be forgotten now while more important things crumbled. The flowers would wilt and turn brown.

Mom followed her gaze. "I'll put it in the fridge, Jenna."

She nodded, even though her cake, preserved or not, had lost its chance to be sliced and passed around in a joyous partaking. Her cake would sit cold behind a door, which would swing open. A light would flash, hunks would be chopped off and sticky handfuls grabbed, until nothing was left on the plate but a pile of crumbs.

❧ 11 ❧

Plans

*T*HE REFRIGERATOR DOOR HAD NO sooner closed on the cake than the telephone rang. Jenna heard her earring click on the receiver as she answered.

"Tomorrow," hummed Kate. "Our big day is tomorrow. Are you in, Jenna?" Kate's voice was quiet, even friendly, but it contained a challenge.

"Of course."

"Wear your very best shorts outfit, and either have pockets or else a purse."

Jenna wasn't sure how to answer with Mom puttering around the kitchen. She didn't have a purse, except for a teeny plastic one that had matched an Easter hat when she was about four.

"And once we get there, you can fix your hair so your earrings show."

"Okay." She was dismayed that she sounded so boring and wondered if she dared ask to use the upstairs phone. Didn't Kate realize that half the

Vander Giffin clan might be hanging over her shoulder? "Where are you going?"

"I?" queried Kate. "Where am *I* going?"

"Kaay-yate!" Jenna strung out the name playfully, as if giggling at an outrageous joke.

"Oh, have you got company?"

"Sure." Jenna said casually as Mom began running dishwater.

"I forgot."

Jenna marveled that Kate could actually forget what it was like to be surrounded by people. She listened closely as Kate rushed on. "It's really very simple. We're going to the mall. Movies, video games, food, shopping, everything. And since this is a Secret Side Day, it's all secret. I'm not asking permission or telling anyone where I'm going. Are you in, Jenna?"

"Sure," Jenna said. She wouldn't have Kate thinking she was a baby.

"No one will notice I'm gone anyway," said Kate. "Do you have a bus schedule at your house?"

"Sure."

"Be here as close to eight as you can. Do you have money?"

This was not something to answer "Sure" to. "I want to earn some money to pay for the hurricane lamp," she said carefully, as Mom turned off the tap and started rattling plates and glasses in the water. It occurred to her suddenly that Mom must be taking someone's turn at dishes. It wasn't her turn Mom was taking; that was for sure. Shooting her mind back to Kate, she hoped Kate would understand that she didn't have money to blow at the mall.

"If you get here early enough, we can walk Fleecy and Woolly before we go. Can you get here before eight? Dogs have to get out kind of early."

"Sure," Jenna said again and almost bit her tongue in annoyance. Couldn't she even vary things by choosing another word? Like *yes*, for instance?

"Have you saved all your money for that woman's lamp?" Kate asked.

"Yes," Jenna said.

"You mean you wouldn't consider spending even a little? When's the last time you bought something?"

"It was a long time ago."

"B.C., huh? Before the Crash?"

"I suppose." Wow, she had thought up another way to say "sure." She had to be more careful though. Her voice had held a grudging tone that time, and soon Mom would be paying more attention than she should.

"Do your parents expect you to save it all?"

Why, they did, didn't they? They might think Lia would want to spend money on paints. They might think David would buy sports magazines or a stash of candy to keep in his sock drawer or his own personal case of pop—and bellow if anyone dared to sneak a can. But what would they expect Jenna to buy? Ingredients for chocolate chip cookies? Things like that were just bought with the groceries. Pens and pencils for writing? There were thousands of them floating around the house—all she had to do was look under the nearest piece of furniture. A new journal? Her old one wasn't filling up very fast lately. No, they would not suppose Jenna would be tempted to spend the money on herself. They would fondly imagine her tucking every nickel in a shoe box to present to them like—ugh—like what Lia had called Sherry a while back, like a puppy.

"Jenna, are you there? Can't you talk? They expect you to save every dime?"

She was not going to say yes to this.

"Being different from what they expect is a good way to have a secret side, you know."

"I know that." Jenna barely kept her voice from snapping. Jenna had invented the phrase secret side, after all. "I know just what you mean, and I have an idea."

"See you in the morning then. Early."

How could the simplest, stupidest, most casual word in the world make her so angry? She said the word anyway. "Okay."

"You and Kate having a difference of opinion?" Mom asked mildly. Jenna was saved from having to answer by Lia's entrance through the back door.

"Hello, family," Lia sang. She swung her head to make her hair billow out unnecessarily far. It settled onto her shoulders in wind-blown waves.

She was not wearing a dab of makeup.

"What's everyone staring at?" she asked.

"You do realize you're late?" Mom still stood at the sink.

Lia gave her dainty shrug. Jenna noticed that even the rounded tops of her shoulders were small and delicate. "I'm sorry." She blinked innocently. "I guess I just didn't plan right. It can't be too late though, can it?" She lifted her finely sculpted chin as if to search the face of the kitchen clock.

At the same moment Cara arrived in the doorway, suddenly bracing her hand on the wood frame as if she'd been running full tilt to the kitchen to witness Lia's arrival. When she saw Lia, a smile spread straight from the center of Cara's mouth and curled the ends. The look she gave Jenna was questioning, then triumphant.

"It's late enough that supper is over." Mom spoke quietly. "Missing the School's-Out Cookout was definitely poor planning. Leaving the dishes for me was poor planning, too."

"Okay!" Lia shrugged again, spread her hands and raised her eyebrows in mock surrender. "I admit I misjudged the time. Isn't that a normal human mistake? Remember when Mrs. Jansen showed up for your Bible study on the wrong day? She apologized for getting her dates mixed up, and you laughed and said it was no big deal—it happens to everybody. Isn't this the same thing?"

"Well, no."

"Why not?" Lia's voice rose dramatically. "You mean only adults have permission to goof up? How come kids have to be perfect? It's just like Mr. Underhill having a fit every time some kid is one nanosecond late for science class, and then in church you find out he's so scatterbrained he misses half his meetings. How come we don't get treated as politely as adults do? How come we have to behave better, when they're the ones everyone says are more responsible?"

"Lia, my concern is that you're trying to pass off deliberate disobedience as a mistake—"

"And they get more privileges!" Lia shouted.

"Even if it was a mistake, the rule is you have to phone us to say you'll be late."

"Oh, now you don't trust me. Besides, how could I call to say I'd be late if I didn't know I was late?"

"I think you're trying to pick a fight." Mom's tone grew clear and firm.

"Pick a fight—"

"Yes. So right now you can either escape the

penalty for missing a chore by taking over these dishes, or you can go up to your room and calm down, and we'll handle this later."

"I'll be upstairs." Lia glided out of the kitchen. Cara flattened herself against the door frame to let her pass.

Mom didn't follow Lia. She didn't yell. She just kept washing Lia's dishes.

Jenna didn't know if Mom's careful, quiet dish-washing made her feel more angry or guilty, but she didn't like either feeling.

"Ha-ha, way to go, Jenna. Lia's gonna come back with makeup on. Yeah, right."

"Yeah, ha-ha," Jenna crabbed to Cara. "You know something? You want to be like Lia, but you sound like Peter."

Cara's face fell for the tiniest instant, and Jenna knew she had hit a nerve. Well, that was fine because she had stuff about herself to worry over, too. What had ever made her think she understood Lia? What possessed her to think that she—dull, routine Jenna—could predict anything about whimsical, theatrical Lia?

Who even cared? Who cared if Mom stood silently at the sink returning good for evil when she could and would be out looking for Sherry if Jenna hadn't had some stupid idea about makeup? Who cared if Cara, only a year and six days younger than she was, thought she was dumb?

Tomorrow was coming, and tomorrow she wouldn't be stupid or dumb. Maybe tomorrow she could change totally. Maybe she wouldn't just sit around mute anymore, having stupid thoughts about how people felt. At the mall all things were new, and just maybe she'd find such a new Jenna that nobody could know her or own her for a long, long time.

❦ 12 ❦

Secret Side Day

*e*ntering the mall's Cafe Court, Jenna found comfort in the noise. Finally, a place where people were talking and moving freely in all directions, and they didn't care if she did the same! She'd heard nothing at home this morning but clicks and squeaks and breathing—and the thud when she'd pitched her journal down between her bed and the wall. Then there'd been that crinkle of paper on the floor when she stepped out of bed. She'd picked it up.

"Sherra. Shera. Sherrah," said the paper. These strange words were followed by a list of names: "Linda. Lia. Jenna. Cara. Maria. Sherra."

Jenna had stared at the paper and at the sheet-draped profile of Sherry in her bed, finally home—the girl who felt she trailed behind and was afraid she might not fit in.

"Malls are so great." Kate's words broke into Jenna's thoughts. Kate looked back and forth happily as they reached the stage area. "We're so early the mall walkers are still here. Are you hungry?"

Jenna's stomach was growling and squirming. She was used to eating breakfast. She patted the pocket of her newest shorts as they strolled to the other end of the mall toward Cinnabon. Quite a bit of Mrs. Geraldine Jarvis's hurricane lamp fund was folded inside this pocket. Who would expect that? Jenna's new shorts, instead of being her usual navy blue, were magenta, and her top was white with huge magenta, gold, and teal blue daisies. Who would expect that? And instead of eggs, toast, or cereal eaten at home, she was about to buy an enormous warm roll with ribbons of cinnamon swirling through it and vanilla frosting drizzling over its edges to make her lick her fingers. Almost as delicious as the roll itself was the knowledge that no one but Kate knew she was eating it.

"There's something I want to buy," said Kate as they strolled from Cinnabon back toward the center of the mall.

A jewelry store with its display of diamond rings in pink-framed windows mounted on marble pedestals caught Jenna's attention. The diamonds, shaped like pears and teardrops, glittered under blinding white lights set into the tops of the glass cases. One ring held a ruby centered in an explosion of tiny colored stones shaped like a peacock's tail.

"You wanna buy this?" Jenna giggled. "It's $9,350!"

"It's gorgeous. But I mean something we really *can* buy."

"Look at the pearl necklaces, Kate. They look all creamy and pinky and—oh, look at this." Standing near the jewelry was a crystal pyramid, flashing stripes of purple, lavender, green, blue, and gold. Lines of fire raced down the edges of the facets as she bent up and down to see the colors swell and shift. "Aren't beautiful things—beautiful? Who buys stuff like this? Kate, somebody has to buy this stuff. My mom wouldn't, or your mom either. So who does? Rich men for their wives?"

"Not at our house. Oh, not that we're so rich," Kate said quickly. "Not rich like that." Kate leaned her forehead on the glass. "I don't know who buys them."

"I'm going to buy beautiful things." Jenna had never had a thought like this before. "Somebody has to. Somebody has to get it out of the store windows and into the houses where people can see it and just feel happy all over that there can be such beautiful things."

"How long would glass triangles last at your house?" Kate's voice was flat.

"Oh. I forgot. But I meant I'm going to buy it

when I'm grown up." Jenna grinned at Kate. "Hey, did you hear what I said? I *forgot* there for a second what our house is like."

"I know what my mom would say." Kate was still gazing at the pyramid, and she didn't turn to Jenna. "The only person who would have that would be somebody without children." Kate straightened up suddenly and seemed to shake herself. "Come on. We've got shopping to do."

"Makeup?" Jenna squealed when Kate finally steered her to an aisle in Target. She'd been disappointed that they weren't going to a smaller, fancier shop, but when Kate had led her into Target she knew Kate was serious about shopping.

"This is beautiful stuff we can afford," Kate said. "I even know what colors to buy 'cause my mom had her colors done once. I need peach and bronze and coral and stuff like that. You need burgundy or deep rose. Or even bright red!"

"Really? I don't even think Lia knows this stuff." The idea that she might get ahead of Lia in the makeup department was thrilling.

Considering all the choices, it took them very little time to select their blush, lipstick, mascara, and eye shadow. But Jenna knew she couldn't look her best without one more item.

"Tweezers?" Kate queried when Jenna pulled it out of her bag in front of the restroom mirror.

"You want to try it?"

"Uh-uh."

"You don't need it anyway." Jenna pinched the tweezers together experimentally once or twice, then tilted her head toward the mirror, and began. Four pulled hairs later there were tears in her eyes. "It hurts!"

"I heard that it does until you get used to it." Kate watched Jenna pluck and wince, occasional pinpricks of blood dotting her brows. "Shouldn't you switch? That one's getting kind of skinny."

"Not skinny enough. But maybe I'll take some off the top." Jenna yanked some hairs along the upper edge of her brow where the pulling seemed less painful. "There. Well . . ." Jenna's voice faded out as she surveyed the results. The eyebrow was thinner but as crooked as a bolt of lightning.

"I just have to even it out," she said with false cheer.

"Don't you think you should start on the other one? You have to make them match. That way you can pick which one looks best and fix the other one to fit." Kate's voice dived to a whisper as two teenage girls entered the rest room. Snapping their gum, they nudged each other and tittered as they fluffed their hair in front of the mirror and filed out again.

"Forget them," said Kate. "Did you see the one

whose mascara was so thick it was practically dripping?"

Jenna had already forgotten everything but her left eyebrow. "I keep pinching my skin," she complained, trying her best to form a graceful arch. "Oh, Kate, this is like art! How come I didn't know that before? I'm horrible at art."

"You want me to try?"

"How many more things am I going to run into in my life that'll turn out to be art when I'm in the middle of them?"

"Are you about done?"

Jenna stopped and inspected the outcome. Her eyebrows looked like something David had done long ago to a couple of fuzzy caterpillars. She was astounded to discover that there was actually a worse kind of eyebrow than thick heavy ones. But she couldn't panic. Saying how awful they were would really make it true. "There must be some makeup that would help." She heard the calm in her voice trying to spread over the horror.

"Have you got a dollar? I'll go buy you an eyebrow pencil." Kate dashed out of the restroom as if she were running from a fire. *Damage this bad*, Jenna thought, *has to be blotted out pronto*. Well, at least now she could argue that she needed makeup. She could not even leave this bathroom until she had it.

"Dark brown," Kate panted, returning. Jenna

snatched the pencil gratefully, uncapping it as if it were life-saving medicine. "Kind of sketch in the—well, bare spots," Kate said apologetically. "I mean, don't use it like a crayon. I'm sorry if this sounds like art."

Jenna decided she might as well sketch since she had already sculpted. Sculpting was the hard part, after all. People said that really good sculptors cut away all the raw material that wasn't part of their art work, until they found the piece of art underneath. Jenna wondered if she was really a bad sculptor or if there was just no art in her eyebrows to be found.

"There." Kate's hands shot out in a stop gesture. "That's it. Not another stroke. You're done."

"They're almost as thick as they were to begin with." Maybe she shouldn't have said that. She didn't want to make that true.

"No, they're not. They're definitely not. Fix your hair so your earrings show now. I'm really so glad you got your ears pierced! Do you think we could change our earrings just for today? We could buy a ton of earrings here and change every hour."

"No, my ears are—still kind of healing." Jenna examined her lobes, trying to look as if she wasn't. She didn't want Kate to ask if they were sore. She thought they were getting better. The border of red around each hole had faded, and there was no dry crusty substance on the earrings. She curved her wiry hair into a kind of shell around each ear, the way she had seen on a TV reporter.

"Great. You've got hair just like a Cabbage Patch Crimp'n Curl doll."

Jenna groaned.

"No, that's good. My mom says you're lucky 'cause your hair has lots of body. Now let's get out of this bathroom. If we decide our makeup needs fixing, we can do it later. We've got plenty of time to experiment until the Big Event."

Jenna fitted her cosmetics into her pocket and faced Kate. "What big event?"

"The—Big—Event." Kate smiled with all of her teeth showing. "But you'll find out about that this afternoon. Until then we shop." Kate swung open the bathroom door, and Jenna followed her out into the milling crowds of the mall.

❧ 13 ❧

The Big Event

THIS IS A CLUE TO THE BIG EVENT," Kate said at the entrance to Pocket Change video arcade.

They went inside, greeted by electronic boops, beeps, and lasers. Rock music throbbed at them from one corner. A row of lights sprayed on from end to end, blinked off, sprayed on again. The game machines divided the floor space into tunnels resembling a maze. Jenna and Kate walked down one of these fingers only to be funnelled into another at its end. Boys of all sizes tugged at joysticks, shot balls, spun steering wheels. There were only a few girls, most of whom were playing an uphill bowling game or hitting mechanical alligators on their heads with mallets. The mallets made a twanging *bow-bow* as they bopped the alligators and sent them retreating into their slots.

"Want to play?" Kate shouted into her ear. "We can get change in the machine over there. When the game's over, we get tickets for our score, and we can spend them on prizes." At that moment a girl carried a string of tickets to the prize counter and handed them over in exchange for an orange-haired troll.

Jenna didn't do very well at the touchdown pass game or the basketball game where the basket kept moving for every shot. The race car track moved too fast for her, and she kept crashing. She couldn't even clobber alligators fast enough to win anything bigger than a pen that smelled like peaches. She'd lost count of how many quarters she had spent, but this was probably the most expensive peach pen anyone had ever owned.

"It doesn't matter." Kate wound two shiny string bracelets around her wrists and put one on her ankle. "Did you pick up the clue to the Big Event? It was there, you know, big as life."

They had double licorice ice cream cones at Bresler's 33 Flavors and then went back to the restroom to repair their lipstick. Jenna jumped when she saw her eyebrows in the mirror. They looked the way Lia might paint them if she did her portrait. Jenna wasn't sure that was good. At least the wet slice of Magenta Magic she added to her mouth balanced her out.

Jenna had been watching her reflection in store windows to see if her eyebrows were shocking. They hadn't seemed too noticeable. It was the fashion magazines that filled a small pocket of her heart with regret. Many of the models had thin brows, of course, but the real surprise was the models with thick, lush brows, even wild brows. Instead of looking quiet and elegant like the skinny-browed ladies, these women looked beautiful in a daring, dangerous way. Why hadn't she ever known there were women who looked like this, who got into fashion magazines, fat eyebrows and all?

They bought lunch at the Dog Haus and sat eating it at Cafe Court, watching the people come and go. One girl appeared to be draped in a lace curtain. A long flowered scarf was tied around her head and flowed like streamers down her back. A young man with black shin-length pants walked through, the sides of his rippling shoulder-length hair drawn up into a rubber band. His black tank top bore the word *MASSACRE* in bent, blood-colored letters.

"Is he famous?" hissed Jenna.

"He's a clue," Kate replied, and she wouldn't say any more.

Jenna's feet began to feel tired as they tramped again through the mall, and around the back of her waist she felt a mild hug of pain that she didn't think had been there before.

It was feeding time at the pet shop. A tiny cocker spaniel buried her whole tiny head in her bowl, curly long ears sweeping the wire floor of her pen. A cairn terrier pawed at the hinges of his cage, spilled his water, and began to bat the dish around. When the aproned attendant came back to refill it, he knocked it over again. A pure white American Eskimo dog yapped incessantly.

"Aren't they cute?" Kate giggled. "I wonder if they'd let a kid buy a dog? I mean, alone?"

"You don't have that much money, do you?"

"Not with me." Kate stared straight into the glass wall that separated the people from the animal cages, just as she had stared at the jewelry. "But I'm saving up kind of a lot at home. Gifts from Dad when he gets home from somewhere. I could get the noisy Eskimo dog." Kate giggled again. Then the smile suddenly fell off her face and left it very straight. "No, I'd get the cocker spaniel. She's a girl, and she looks a little sad, and she's so small you could hug all of her at once."

Jenna looked longingly at the dogs, wishing she could pet them. She loved their bright eyes, their fur, their springy tails. She didn't think she'd want the cairn terrier though. All the spilling, pawing, and wacky behavior were already too plentiful at her house.

"Any clues there?" Jenna asked as they exited.

"Not really." Kate's voice was listless at first and then perked up. "In just a roundabout way, I guess. Wait. There!" Kate jabbed her finger straight out in front of her. "There is a clue."

Jenna saw nothing but T-shirts, columns and rows of them on a four-sided display that reached far above her head. "I'm not forty," one announced. "I'm eighteen with twenty-two years experience." All of these shirts were either about getting old or loving chocolate. Then a plain black and white one caught her eye. "Property of Jesus," it proclaimed. It was a Christian shirt that had gone out into the T-shirt world to tell other shirts about Jesus. Jenna blinked and shook away this weird thought.

"You don't mean these dumb T-shirts are a clue?" Jenna asked.

"No. There."

Kate was pointing to a life-size cardboard statue of a boy wearing a jacket, jeans, and athletic shoes. A sign he was holding said, "Need help? This way to service stop." His message was no more exciting than the T-shirts, and Jenna had no idea what Kate meant.

"Just how much longer till the Big Event?" Jenna wanted to know. She was getting seriously tired of walking. The shop in front of them which sold wooden crafts was boring. She could not imagine who would want to buy wooden watermelon.

"It's time," Kate said. "This means back to the bathroom to fix our makeup."

In front of the mirror, Jenna stroked more mauve eye shadow on her lids. "Okay now, what is the Big Event?"

"You won't get hyper?" Kate fluffed her hair with her pick.

Jenna looked at her in surprise. She suddenly felt as if she were being tested again. "What do you mean?"

"Well, maybe it's only fair to warn you." Kate tucked her cinnamon-colored blush back into her pocket. "But maybe you'll panic and get nervous and sweaty." Kate studied her, and the feeling of being judged by her best friend filled Jenna with horror.

"I will not," Jenna declared.

"Maybe you won't." Kate tilted her head and tapped one of Jenna's earrings with her fingernail. "We have to go to Cafe Court," Kate told her as they left the restroom. "So maybe I'll tell you on the way. Promise you won't freak—oh, there they are. It's too late. Just come with me, keep cool, and you look fine." Kate raised one hand in a graceful wave. "Craig?"

A boy turned to Kate, a boy just as cute as the cardboard model. His jeans, shoes, and shirt were absolutely up to the minute in fashion. His jaw was strong. His freshly washed hair, palest brown but flashing gold where the light hit it, brushed his forehead appealingly. Jenna knew the type. This was a coolest-athlete-in-the-fifth-grade kind of guy, the first boy in his crowd to have a girlfriend. And his girlfriend was always the cutest, most popular—his girlfriend was always someone like Kate!

"Craig, this is my friend Jenna." Kate flashed her winningest smile and spread it to include them both. Jenna knew Kate was telling her several things with that smile. She was saying, *Please be fun, Jenna. Don't spoil it for me. I'm going to trust you not to act stupid and run and disappoint me now, okay?*

"And, Justin, this is my friend Jenna. Jenna, this is Justin."

A shorter, darker boy stepped out of Craig's shadow. "Hi."

"Hi," Jenna returned, her voice wobbling.

"Well, should we look around?" Kate asked brightly, as if she and Jenna hadn't been doing that for the past five hours. Jenna felt a tug of dismay to see Kate stroll slightly ahead with Craig. She seemed to have plenty to say to him, too.

Justin took one last quizzical look at Jenna— she was afraid it was at her eyebrows—before they more or less fell into step behind the friends who had brought them here. *That's pretty much the truth of it, too,* Jenna thought as a flash of insight she didn't really want lodged itself in that secret pocket of her heart. She had come along with Kate. This trip to the mall had been Kate's thing. Justin had come along with Craig, maybe at Kate's suggestion.

"You want somethin' to eat?" Craig had turned to Jenna and Justin, walking backwards, and his eyes now caught Jenna's. Her stomach dipped nervously. With all she'd already had to eat she didn't think she'd be hungry till Monday, but it was something to do, and it was good to be agreeable. She managed a nod and felt better when the four of them drifted closer together.

Kate beamed as Craig paid for four saucer-size chocolate-chunk-and-nut cookies. The two of them strolled ahead again, nibbling, Jenna and Justin following as they approached a stand of cheeses, sausages, and fancy boxed cakes.

"Hey, let's get out of here—" Justin began.

Craig's arm swung out as he passed the cheeses. At least Jenna thought it did; his elbow moved, and the edge of his jacket brushed the table.

"—I'm allergic to weeds," Justin finished.

The musty, sweetish smell of a dried flower and herb shop tickled her nose. Had that space of bare white table among the cheeses been there before Craig passed? Did she see what she thought she saw? Justin's talking had distracted her.

Kate pulled down suddenly on Craig's other arm.

Jenna heated up like a furnace. *Did he steal some cheese? He couldn't have. I'm just seeing things.* She wondered if anyone else had seen. But she knew no one had. She herself had covered him from the rear.

"Craig!" Kate said. Or at least Jenna thought that was what she said. It was hard to tell with Kate walking ahead.

Craig mumbled something about crackers.

"Craig!" Kate wailed.

They stopped, half-turned to Jenna and Justin, Kate still clutching at Craig's hand.

"Hey, how about if we cut out of here." Craig looked mostly at Justin, but his look brushed over Jenna, too. "This walkin' around gets to be a drag in no time."

"Oh, that would be great!" Kate's voice was almost shrill, and she twisted and pulled Craig's fingers as if she were milking a cow. "Let's go, Jenna. We've seen it all anyway."

Panic bubbled up from Jenna's stomach. She felt sick from the queasiness, the food, and the fear of what she was about to say. But she said it anyway.

"I don't want to."

She felt wide open, as if fences were being taken away. The mall was her frame for this day, and she wanted to keep it.

"Aw, come on, Jenna. It's time we got outside." Kate's confident smile was back.

"No, Kate, please." Jenna heard her own whining, the childishness. But she didn't want Kate to change this much.

"Jenna, come on! It'll be great; you'll see. We can walk around or take a bus wherever we want."

"Hey, if she doesn't wanna—" Justin began.

"Jenna, I thought you'd be up for this," Kate complained. "When you got your ears—" She sighed. "But I was right to begin with. You're not ready." Kate turned to Craig.

"Want to go?" He asked so casually. He knew he'd won.

"Yes," said Kate, but she was drowned out by a furious soprano.

"Jenna Lynn Vander Giffin!"

Jenna's stomach jerked yet again, and she whirled to face . . . Lia.

Her sister wore a shell-pink beaded sweater, black stirrup pants, and soft black slippers. Her eyes were outlined, fringed, and shadowed in fuchsia. She wore lipstick and blush and probably foundation, and she had to have gone to a salon to get her hair curled and fluffed to the width of a fancy Barbie doll's.

Sensations churned through Jenna. *Copycat! No, she'll say I copied. Hey, I was right about Lia and the makeup—I was just a day early!* She felt a flash of anger, a gulp of silliness, a chin lifted in equality, that in the next second fell as low as Craig's. *He's gawking at her. Lia is gorgeous.*

Lia showed no mixture of emotion and took no notice of Craig. Her eyes and mouth were squinted into tight angry buds.

"Lia Kaye Vander Giffin," Jenna returned.

Their eyes spit and shot sparks. Kate, Craig, and Justin waited for the show, but Jenna and Lia had no words to fight with that couldn't be hurled right back at each other. They trembled with the hot lava of built-up anger. If she screamed, Jenna thought, if she lunged—maybe today Mrs. Geraldine Jarvis was picking up her replacement hurricane lamp at J. C. Penney and would waddle past with her box at that exact moment . . . Jenna realized with a sinking feeling that they stood only ten paces from that store. It was like some kind of sign. The Lord.

Suddenly, Lia came alive, playing her winning card. "You have no eyebrows!"

"Kate!" A woman's voice flew at them from behind and was overlapped by a man's. "Kate!"

Jenna turned to see Mr. and Mrs. Schmidt running toward them, foreheads creased, mouths gaping.

"My parents," Kate murmured, amazed. "They're together."

"Oh man," said a boy's voice faintly, behind them now. Jenna couldn't tell which one it was.

"Jenna!"

Jenna looked past the Schmidts and thought she might collapse. Hurrying toward her, braid flying, was Mom. Trotting beside Mom, the wooden cross he wore on a chain about to take a dive over his left shoulder, was Dad.

"Let's cut," a boy's muted voice said, again from behind her.

The Vander Giffins and Schmidts were running through the mall! Toward J. C. Penney! Now Jenna felt sure Mrs. Geraldine Jarvis wasn't here today. It couldn't happen to adults. But who did Mom have in tow? It was Sherry!

"Praise the Lord!" Mrs. Schmidt exploded, reaching them first.

"What happened to your two friends?" asked Kate's dad.

Jenna did not have to turn around to know that Craig and Justin were gone.

❧ 14 ❧

Lost and Found

"JENNA, HOW COULD YOU DO THIS?" Mom looked at Jenna helplessly and burst into tears.

"Kate! We were worried sick."

"And Lia. Lord, I don't understand what's going on." Mom put a hand over her eyes. "With any of them."

Sherry looked from Lia to Jenna and back again, head darting like a small animal, hair flicking. "You got in trouble?"

"It's about trust," Mom was saying, her weeping leveling off. "You want freedom. Don't you know that you give up freedom when you lose our trust? Do you kids know how much you affect us? Do you know you have the power to hurt us?"

And then something fell away from Jenna. She suddenly felt taller, as if her lungs could expand better. In the secret pocket of her heart she felt . . . significant. And the funny thing was—maybe it was too late. Maybe Mom and Dad were going to clamp down now harder than ever.

"Did you do it on purpose?" Sherry's face was lighted by something like wonder, or hope. Was she hoping they had? *No*, Jenna thought, *she wants to know. It means something to her.*

Sherry looked at her then, and Jenna knew Sherry saw the obvious answer. "Your eyebrows are gone."

Jenna's face suddenly felt gooey in places, dry and cracked in others. Inside she wished her makeup would just slide off.

"Mom and Dad had to come and get you," Sherry said. But she was looking at her parents, not at her sisters.

"That's right," Dad said carefully, clearly. "Just as we had to come and get you. Just the same."

They'd gotten Sherry from somewhere, of course. Jenna remembered. This morning she'd been back in her bed. She too had been searched for and found, just as the lost sheep had been found by the shepherd in the Bible who had ninety-nine others to care for. And if he'd lost two more the very next day—he would have gone after them, too.

Sherry stood tall, and Jenna found herself hoping Sherry's shrug was gone for good. "I am a Christian too," she said, and Dad's and Mom's hands crept up to her shoulders.

They'd be hauled home now. There'd be another awful supper and a talk, and they'd have to confess what they'd done wrong so Mom and Dad were sure they understood.

"I blame myself for this."

Jenna looked up in surprise to see Kate's dad, Mr. Schmidt, standing with them. She had the sudden feeling he'd repeated this several times at the edges of her hearing.

His skin looked pale. Deep lines gouged his face between his nose and mouth, and even his red hair seemed to have faded to the color of weak tea. "I've really gotten away from the Lord." He straightened himself somewhat. "Look, I should probably say this. Mark and Linda—I've had time on the way over here to think—" He rubbed his head tiredly. "I feel like God just hit me with a two-by-four. I've put my job ahead of my family." He sighed. "Way far ahead." He glanced at his wife and then turned back and faced the children. "I've disobeyed. I've disobeyed God. Disobedience adds up. Whether it's one person or a whole group of people, it seems that disobedience spills over until it messes up everything. I'm not sure how to change. I'm so dug in at work that I'm not sure how to climb out. But there must be a way."

Emotions tugged at Jenna. She wasn't sure she liked Mr. Schmidt claiming her Secret Side Day was started by him. But the idea that an adult could disobey, and say so, gave her the strange sensation that sections of the floor were moving up and down, evening them out.

The desire to remind her parents that they'd been running in the mall died inside her.

She wanted to wash her face.

Kate's parents were drawing her away. "Can I talk to Jenna first?" she asked faintly. "Can I talk to Jenna a minute?" Kate asked Mom.

They sat on a bench, hunched behind a potted tree, wanting to hide inside the crowd of shoppers that filed back and forth on either side of them. "I told you a lie. I did see you here that day—the day the hurricane lamp got broke."

Jenna looked at Kate. "Why did you say you didn't? Why did you run?"

"I can't tell you." Kate stared at a faraway point, and she shoved hair behind her ear again as she had that day when she was poised to flee. "I was so afraid you were going to find out what I did. That's why I ran, but I can't tell you any more. It's just too awful. But it's over, and no way will I do it again." She paused abruptly. "I mean lie or the other thing. The reason I had to run." She took a breath. "I'm sorry I lied. I'm sorry you saw me and thought I didn't like you anymore or something. And I'm really sorry you ran into Mrs. Jarvis because of me. Listen." Kate snapped her

146

head toward Jenna, looking fierce. "I'll tell you a secret. This is top-bunk stuff. Okay?"

"Okay," Jenna said.

"My dad is right. About disobedience spilling and messing stuff up. You caught me doing something wrong, and it didn't have anything to do with you, but all of a sudden it *did* have something to do with you because there you were, and you got the wrong idea. I did some stupid thing and almost wrecked our friendship at the same time, and there was no way in the world I could have known that might happen. It's like . . ." She paused. "If you get mixed up with wrong stuff, it can steal from you. It takes away stuff you didn't know you might lose." Kate squirmed. "Is that stupid?"

"No," Jenna said, thoughts whirling.

"You have to understand about Craig. He's cool. I mean, he has all these friends. He's the star basketball player. All the girls drool over him." Kate paused. "And his parents are divorced. But he's still cool." She looked away. "Do you know what I mean?"

Jenna nodded. "I mean, yes."

Kate had needed to see Craig's secret side where he stored the secret of being cool and okay even when his parents were divorced. But—maybe Craig wasn't so okay after all. And maybe that had nothing to do with divorce, but it still scared Kate.

Kate was wiping her eyes, opening them wide,

stretching away any signs of crying. "Outside, walking around, hanging around, he's always nice. He's cool. I was never at the mall with him before."

Jenna nodded.

"I gotta go."

Kate left the mall without looking back. Watching her go, Jenna knew Kate was shattered. Yet she left the mall between her parents, wrists tucked up under the crooks of two strong arms.

It was with blessed relief that Jenna realized, moments later, her thoughts had become prayer.

❦

"I had no idea Rob and Julie's marriage was in trouble." Mom and Dad headed across the mall parking lot with Lia, Sherry, and Jenna. "I'm just sick. I mean about not knowing. We're supposed to be friends with them, and here they are hiding from all of us because they think they're not perfect enough or holy enough or something."

"Well, it sounds like they started to communicate in a hurry when they realized Kate was missing," Dad said. "Which is one good thing." Dad turned to Jenna. "Mrs. Schmidt was the one who realized Kate was so keen on the mall lately, and she thought you might have come here together. Lia we knew we'd find here. But you—we didn't know."

She, Jenna the predictable, was the one whose

whereabouts her parents couldn't guess. She remembered Sherry suddenly. Where and how had they found *her* after she'd left home? How well had Sherry stumped them?

"I got my ears pierced," Jenna said.

They reached the car. No one spoke as they got in, rolled down the windows, and buckled their belts. Then Mom turned.

"Tell me, were you trying to rebel in every way you could think of all in one day?"

"No, I wanted a secret side—" Jenna jerked her eyes away from Mom.

Mom seemed to need no explanation. "A secret side. And you thought," she said in quiet disbelief, "you didn't have one?" Her voice rose. "You thought *you* didn't have one?" No one spoke.

"I guess I don't know you as well as I thought." Mom's tone was not scolding. It was gentle and respectful and was more shocking to Jenna than the words. Mom faced the front again as Dad guided the car through the labyrinth that was the mall parking lot.

These were the very words Jenna longed for, the very words she wanted to be true. Funny that they stung her as much as they pleased her.

"I didn't get them pierced today. It was more than two weeks ago."

"I don't believe this," Lia exploded. "She got her ears pierced before I did. She plucks her eye-

149

brows till they look like a dead spider's legs and then scribbles on them with crayon. She even has a date. And you don't even yell." She turned to Jenna. "I actually confided in you. But you're a double-crosser. I guess I don't know you either."

A date? The idea made her feel a bit giddy, but she rejected it. A date was special. She would not waste her first date on something as stupid as walking in the mall next to a boy she didn't know.

"Lia, I don't think Jenna's ear-piercing and makeup had much to do with you," Mom said. "You girls all think about how everything affects you."

"Now will you please take a look at how you've affected each other," Dad added. "And all of us."

For a few moments no one spoke.

"She should have to grow them shut," Lia said. "It's only fair."

"Nooo." Mom sounded thoughtful. "Mark, if you agree, I'm inclined to go home and tell them they can all get their ears pierced. It's just not important enough to be a bone of contention."

Jenna had never heard of a bone of contention before, but she was pretty sure it meant a thing to fight over. She was amazed.

"Isn't Jenna getting away—" Dad began, but Lia drowned him out.

"She's getting away with murder!"

"I'm not so sure," Mom said. "Lia, I'm sorry if

you think it's unfair. You were the first to get permission. I'm afraid some of this is just part of being the oldest. I was the oldest sister in my family, too, and it seemed every time I got to do something Deb and Pam were right behind me getting to do it, too. Parents practice on older ones. Parents get wiser." She paused. "Parents get tired."

"Lia, suppose we made you return the clothes you bought at the mall today," Dad said. "How would you feel?"

"Mad!"

"Right. And would you try to get back at us some other way?"

Lia didn't answer.

"Mom and I don't need to create a power struggle. If Jenna keeps her pierced ears, she'll remember this day and whatever she learned from it for the rest of her life."

Jenna supposed that was true. Now that Dad had said so, the whole day and this whole ride home were probably printed on her brain forever. Dad had seen something inside her, but he hadn't seen it all. He didn't know that her need to strain at the boundaries seemed to be gone. That was a most private secret for the pocket of her heart.

❧ 15 ❧

The Secret Side

BLUE DUSK HAD FALLEN, THE DEEP gray-blue that never quite got to navy before black stamped it out. Jenna pulled down the shades in her room, turning when she heard footsteps. Sherry stood in the doorway. "You got grounded."

Jenna nodded.

Sherry nodded with her, satisfied. "Me too."

"Just like me and Lia," Jenna said slowly. "Just the same . . . Sherry, you don't have to answer if you don't want. But can I ask you a secret side thing?"

"What?" Sherry came into the room and closed the door.

"Where did you go . . . yesterday?" Jenna's voice fell to almost a whisper. "Where were you when Dad found you?"

Sherry stood looking at her for a moment. Then she sat on her bed. "I was at our house."

"Our . . . house?"

"Me and my mom's house. On Lincoln Street.

We lived there when I was a baby. I found that out in my Life Book."

"No kidding." Jenna was amazed. "You used to live on Lincoln Street? Where?"

"Way out." Sherry waved her arm vaguely. "Almost out of town. It's a big, kind of purply house."

"Oohh." Jenna closed her mouth carefully. She knew just the house Sherry meant—a falling-down maroon place with a front porch like a see-saw and a jungle of spiny bushes.

"I hid under the porch," Sherry said. "But they kept calling and calling. Dad even crawled under. I felt so funny with him laying there in the dirt that I came out." She shrugged.

Suddenly Jenna felt she could hear the voices calling Sherry's name, see the arms reaching under the porch, the fingers wiggling and beckoning. It was as if Sherry had finally crawled out from the gravel and weeds and got in the car, finally believed she could go with them, because the family had come back to her old life to get her, claim her, and carry her into the new.

"They told me . . ." Sherry said, "they told me I could treasure my Life Book forever."

After Sherry left the room, Jenna turned her bed covers down. They stuck on the wall side, and as she dug at the spot where her comforter bunched up, Jenna's fingers knocked a book down the wall. Even though the rough plaster scraped her knuckles, she hauled out her journal. To her surprise a note stuck above the flowered cover.

Dear Jenna,

> *I've never read your journal, and I never will. But do you think maybe there's a secret side in here?*
> *In Matthew 10 Jesus says if we find a life for ourselves that's more important than He is, we lose our real life. Then He says if we give up that life for His sake, we find our life. That may be kind of hard to understand, but you already know that today's kind of secret side can't last. You have another secret side that is always with you. Please think about what that may be.*

Love,
Mom

Jenna opened her journal, the journal that no one but she had ever read.

> *Special giant thank You for Kate . . .*
> *Jesus, no one knows how I feel about books. Big thick books make me kind of hungry. I want to take bites out of them . . .*
> *Lord, I studied my brains out. Please help me pass the math test . . .*
> *I'm boring. Everybody thinks they own me. I'm going to find a secret side and keep it all to myself.*

The page held a few more stray words, even half

a sentence. Then the flow of navy-blue ink stopped. The following pages were lined, ready, prompting. But they were blank.

She switched on her bedside lamp and found a pen.

Dear Jesus,

I'm sorry. I didn't write for a long time because I gave up my journal when I tried to find a secret side. All it turned out to be was a trip to the mall and a bunch of stuff that would have to stop once Mom and Dad found out. The money for Mrs. G. J. and her H. L. would have run out. Now I have to earn it back. Even my eyebrows will grow back. I want them to though. I'll feel like I'm back to normal.

You and I can really talk in my journal, and that's a secret side and a real life. Talking about secret stuff is not just for kids. Grownups do it all the time.

I think this has something to do with that Scripture Mom wrote in her note. I'm not sure I get it, but I bet sometime You'll explain. It's okay if You don't right away. You can take as long as You like.

I just noticed that Jenna and journal fit together. They both start with J. And Jenna and Jesus have the same number of letters!

Thanks for forgiving me.

Love,
Jenna

❧ 16 ❧

Epilogue

ON FRIDAY, THE TWENTY-SIXTH OF
June, Sherry Ann Johnson donned a lilac
dress of silk crepe, sewn by her mother, and before
a smiling Circuit Court judge became Sherry Ann
Johnson Vander Giffin.

Jenna had expected vows. Certainly Sherry's
peaceful face under her shiny, soft haircut,
between her delicate pink earrings, showed will-
ingness to take them. But the judge only asked a
few questions. Only Sherry's clear, confident pro-
nouncement of her name, Sher*ry*, seemed anything like a ceremony.

As Jenna watched the family pass Sherry
around through a dance of hugs and high fives,
grandmotherly tears and boyish smiles, she understood. Vows weren't needed today. Sherry had
grown into the family as they all had and was
rooted down deep, even through the wandering

and the secrets. Today was a solemn, joyous cele-
bration of the work that God had done.

❦

The Riverside Supper Club had a huge, round
table set into its own alcove. One by one the
Vander Giffins entered and scurried to the inside,
making room also for Grandma and Grandpa
Schellenburg and for their social worker, Laurie
Joseph.

Jenna ate her juicy, tender-as-butter steak until
she had to sink back, stuffed. She rested until
mounded napkins, pushed-back plates, and dog-
gie bags signaled the end of the feast. She sat up
straight when the waitress said, "Dessert?"

In the middle of the cleared white tablecloth sat
a stack of plates, a silver cake server, and a small
layer cake frosted in white, trimmed with a green
trellis and leaf design, topped by a nosegay of
wildflowers.

Jenna's eyes found Mom's. "Did you . . . did
they make . . ."

Mom shook her head. "It's yours. I froze the top
layer. Would you like to do the honors, Jenna?"

Hands guided the cake and the plates her way.
"Cut 'em small."

Jenna cut thin slices of cake, the zesty spices filling her nostrils.

"Just a sliver for me, please."

Jenna lifted them high with the beautiful cake server, sliding them onto the plates.

"If I eat one more bite, I'm gonna bust."

Jenna took the nosegay from the top of the cake, placed it on the first slice, and set it in front of Sherry. Joyfully she continued cutting and passing until she'd given her entire cake away.

"Sherry has something to share with you."

The family hushed as Laurie Joseph and Sherry, standing together, placed five tall white candles, in silver holders, on the table. Sherry struck a match and lit one.

"What does the candle mean?" Laurie asked softly.

"This is the Jesus candle."

"Why do you call it the Jesus candle?"

"Because," Sherry said, her solemn gaze focusing on the flame, "He loved us first." Sherry picked up a second candle, dipped it, and lit it off the first.

"What candle is that?"

"This is me."

"And that means . . ."

"I can love because He loved me." Sherry lit the third candle from her own. "This is the Chris Johnson candle. She's the person I loved first."

Silence reigned around the table. The candles burned quietly, steadily. Then came the fourth candle. "This is the Jernigans, my first foster family. I loved them too. They couldn't take me when they moved, but that's okay now."

Jenna thought of Sherry's secret side, what it must hold, what things must be inside people to make them act in ways she didn't understand. She thought of Kate.

Sherry was lighting the fifth candle, dipping its wick to the center of the flame on her own. "This," she said, "is the Vander Giffin candle. My new family." Her voice dropped. "I love them, too."

Flame shadows flickered and danced on the wall. Slowly, Sherry set the candle down. The five candles glowed together, their flames straight and reaching high.

Watching them, Jenna longed to light candles, too. She would hand them around the table to all of her family. But these candles, this moment, belonged to Sherry. If only she could just have a Jesus candle . . .

But she did. Though it stood in front of Sherry, the same one would do for her. They all had Him, and He knew all their secret sides, and He shone on their dark parts until they all had their very own secret sides of light.

Raising her hands, the candle flames suddenly blurring before her eyes, Jenna joined her family in the applause.